Underland Arcana continues its deep exploration of our mercurial psyches with stories about what lurks in wells, yards, and the future. Stories about how we piece together our histories. Stories about wishes and witches, and the scientific intersection of both. Stories about how we hide our fears in plain sight, and oh, indeed, stories about running from those same fears. This issue may be all about reflections.

Underland Arcana is published quarterly. This issue is published in conjunction with the new moon that slips across the edge of the world and creeps across a new sky.

EDITOR
Mark Teppo

COVER IMAGE
thanawong

SIGIL ART
Andrew Penn Romine

PUBLISHER
Underland Press
Clackamas, OR, USA

Up before the sun, across the fields while the dew is still fresh . . .

https://www.underlandarcana.com

UNDERLAND ARCANA

~ 07 ~

Underland Press

Contents

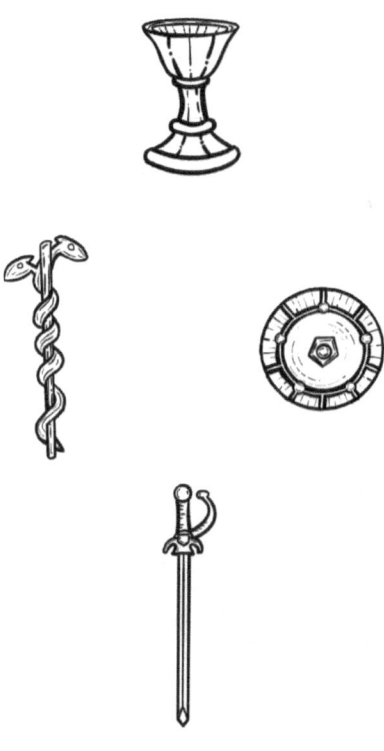

Happy Little Trees

I'm sure you know of the famous landscape painter who was both mocked and celebrated for his inveterant delight at his creative process, and how he always managed a little whimsey and magic in his pictures. One of the stories in this issue reminds me of his happy little aphorism about painting—a reminder which I am sure the author intends us to reflect on—and this led me to source a cover image that would play to that story.

This isn't my normal process because a) sourcing art to match a story is always a huge pain in the ass (though, circumventing that process did lead to one of my fruitful collaborations back in the day), and b) if you start with art and put out the ask for stories that play to that art, you run the risk of having a whole issue filled with like-minded stories. While that's fine and dandy, it's not exactly the model that I'm building Arcana on.

(I say this being completely aware that I'm going to eat these words in about six issues, but bridges and crossings and all that.)

Anyway, issue 7 continues the fish theme, but yes, we've added a tiny little house. It might be a happy house. I'll leave that up to you. Otherwise, here we are: over halfway through the second year of *Arcana*. I'm delighted to make it pass six issues, and we look forward to, well, some vague number more.

I've been sending individual tarot cards to each subscriber with their issues. The idea is that, eventually, they will all have a complete deck of unique cards. Of course, that is seventy-eight cards, and at four issues a year, that is <counts on fingers> nearly twenty years, taking us through 2040.

I'll be . . . old.

This might be an unsustainable idea. But whatever. Part of the joy of the creative act is showing up and creating. Let's enjoy ourselves now. At least the sky's not on—oh, wait.

Mark Teppo
June 12th, 2022

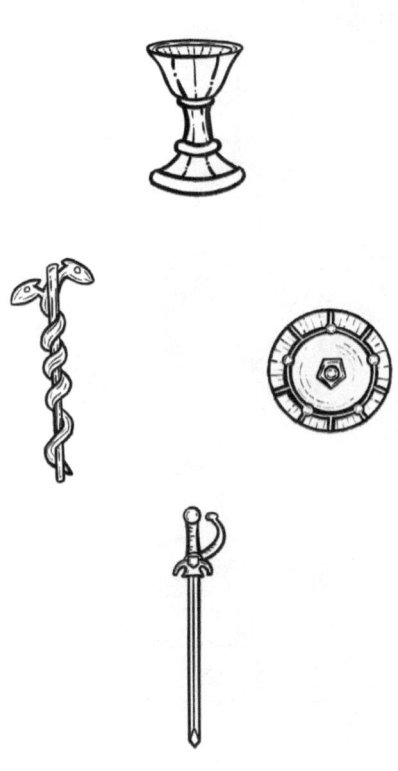

KNIGHT of CUPS.

Bones Placed in Apposition

~ A. P. Howell

Featherstonhaugh glanced upward at the old State House. Lukens's new four-sided clock was an impressive feat of engineering, but there was something to the criticism of its legibility at a distance, especially when the sun was bright and the viewer's eyes less sharp than a young man's. The steeple's white paint stood out brilliantly against a cloudless sky, and the clock confirmed Featherstonehaugh was on time for his appointment. He crossed Chestnut Street, avoiding horse droppings with an ease borne of extended periods of urban living.

He stood now in the heart of Philadelphia, which was—or at least had been—the heart of the new country. On the corner, City Hall bustled with the thousand and one tasks necessary to maintain a city of eighty thousand souls. When Featherstonhaugh had first arrived in the city, the Supreme Court had but lately relocated to the new capital, and the locals had often lapsed into calling the building the "old courthouse" or "new city hall." Across Fifth Street sat the Library Company of Philadelphia, soon to be celebrating its centennial.

Featherstonhaugh's destination was a brick building standing proudly beside City Hall on Fifth Street: Philosophical Hall. One of many noble institutions shepherded into existence by Franklin and like-minded contemporaries, the American Philosophical Society was a jewel of American intellectual life. It was devoted not merely to the acquisition of learned volumes, in the manner of the Library Company, but to expanding knowledge on all manner of subjects.

This was a worthy goal in general, but particularly necessary in America. An entire continent of mysteries laid waiting for discovery and documentation. As rich as European intellectual society might be, correspondence could go only so far. Home-grown intellectuals were needed to advance knowledge, solve problems particular to the United States, and make use of its natural resources.

"Good afternoon!" Hays called as Featherstonhaugh stepped inside. He waited on the second floor, leaning against the banister and looking entirely comfortable in this temple of learning.

"I am most happy we found a mutually agreeable time." Featherstonhaugh did not whisper as he ascended, but pitched his voice politely low. A murmur of voices from behind closed doors indicated a university class in session or some other consultation. The other man had not precisely been rude—especially if he happened to know the other conversation was of little consequence—but Featherstonhaugh chose to err on the side of propriety.

Hays was a medical man in his thirties. Featherstonhaugh understood he had formerly been involved in his family's East India trade, but had apparently found himself ill-suited to the work. He had developed something of a name as a natural scientist and had literary ambitions, having already produced writing in the medical field. He was unmarried, a fact Featherstonhaugh could not help but look upon with a hint of suspicion and pity. He wondered a bit at the temperament of a man who had not yet settled into matrimony.

By Hays's age, Featherstonhaugh had been a new father, married for half a decade. Memories of Sally still pained him. Thoughts of his boys brought forth painful details of the girls' final days. Instead, he considered Charlotte, her genteel upbringing and charming Virginia accent.

Languages had always been among Featherstonehaugh's interests. If not for his fascination in the subject, he would not have come to America, would not have settled here (*settled*: that was true, and infinitely safer than *met Sally*). He would not have met Charlotte with her charming accent and the youth that was lost to him, and would have neither needed nor found a second chance at domestic life.

Thoughts of mortality brought him round to the reason it was Hays ushering him into a second floor room, and not the author of the article that had caught his interest.

"I am sorry to have missed Godman's lecture, and sorrier for his passing," Featherstonhaugh said. "He had been ill for some time, I believe?"

Hays nodded. "But though it did not come as a surprise, he still passed too young. He will be missed. His mind is a great loss to the medical community, and to America's natural historians."

"His *Transactions* paper piqued my interest. A new genus and species of elephant . . . it is a bold claim."

"So Harlan says," Hays noted. "He also believed he described Lewis and Clark's Iowa fossil adequately, before I corrected his work with my *Saurodon*. He cannot be said to understand reptiles, for all the words he writes on the subject, much less mammals. And were Godman here, I am certain he would remind you of the man's plagiarism."

Featherstonhaugh shrugged, suspecting that Godman would have a good deal more to say on the subject of Harlan. Philadelphia's natural historians' opinions about one another were no less passionate than their opinions on scientific matters. "That is why I wish to see the specimen myself. As masterful as Peale's illustrations may be, there is something to be said for direct observation."

Hays unlocked a cabinet. "The vertebrae, ribs, and bones of the limbs are available for your examination as well, and may be of interest since illustrations did not accompany Godman's article. But you are no doubt here for these." Hays carefully transferred the skull and jaw fragments to a table.

The largest intact section of the upper jawbone was seventeen inches in length. Five inches of upper tusk rested within their sockets, with another twelve inches exposed on the right side and ten on the left. A good seven and a half inches in circumference where they emerged from the socket, the tusks did not begin to narrow to a point until the final four inches of their length. The patterns of wear had been represented to a fair degree of accuracy in Peale's illustrations.

Featherstonhaugh paid particular attention to the lower jaw, the formation of which had so strongly captured Godman's attention. It was indeed dramatically elongated at the extremity, the angles more rectangular than the curvature he had observed in other mastodon specimens. A full three inches of tusk rested in the socket; the exposed portion, about one inch in length, was covered with black enamel and ended with a spiral twist. He pressed a thumbnail into dry, grayish bone of the tusk and felt it yield.

"It is similar to the mastodon," Featherstonhaugh said, "as Godman himself noted. The wear upon the milk teeth reveals only surface enamel, as in the mastodon, not the elephant . . ."

"Not any elephant heretofore known," Hays said.

Featherstonhaugh continued to examine the lower jaw. "They are, without doubt, milk teeth. Godman is certainly correct in his assertion that this is a juvenile animal."

"Yes, that is quite clear."

Featherstonhaugh frowned, more at the prickliness creeping into the other man's tone than at any feature of the long-dead animal before him, and squinted at the sockets of the tusks. "The elongation of the jaw is indeed interesting."

"If I may." Hays reached into a pocket to produce a pair of spectacles. "These may be of some use."

A. P. Howell

Featherstone set the jawbone carefully upon the table. "Do you mean to insult my observations? Or have you invented lenses to ease the work of natural scientists?"

"More the latter," Hays said, in pale imitation of Featherstonhaugh's attempted jocularity. "I seek to work at the forefront of ophthalmology. Our eyes fail, whether through disease or age or mischance. But with research, skill, and the proper diagnosis and intervention, what has gone wrong may be put right."

Featherstonhaugh took the spectacles, always interested in the state of scientific advances. The frames were wire, functional, and sturdy; though hardly fashionable, neither were they unnecessarily unattractive. The lenses themselves appeared well-made, which was unsurprising with the resources at Hays's disposal. With a casual examination, Featherstonhaugh could not discern the lenses' intent; there was none of the distortion one might expect in a pair of spectacles made to correct either far-sightedness or myopia.

He hooked them over his ears, expecting the blurriness of wearing another's spectacles, but his vision remained unchanged. If not for the visible wire of the frames within his field of view, he would not have known he wore them. He wondered if this was some joke of Hays's, or if the man's skill did not extend to lens-grinding. But Featherstonehaugh's concern about politic statements were rendered moot.

Hays lifted the upper and lower jaws, one in each hand. This seemed unnecessarily cavalier: though the lower jaw was only one foot in length, the upper jaw was half again as long and further unbalanced by twelve inches of tusk. Featherstonhaugh wondered if he was to play witness to a careless loss to natural history and a strike to Hays's reputation.

But Hays proved dexterous and settled the jaws together as they would have met in life. The right side of the head was, as promised in Godman's text and Peale's plates, in excellent condition. Held together, Featherstonhaugh could see the animal as it would have been in life, a youngster more kin to elephants than mastodons, and utterly (if subtly) distinct from all other known species. *Tetracauldodon mastodontoideum.*

He imagined layers of muscle and flesh and fur, tendons snaking between bones, those jaws opening and closing. He extrapolated the rest of the body, and after that the effects of maturity. But for whatever mischance had killed the beast, it would have grown to adulthood. He could picture it striding across the continent with its fellows. This one had died in Orange County, and why would it not have roamed Featherstonehaugh's old estate? Tromping over hills and fields yet to be planted, a place where one day a house would be built, sheep imported, fields tilled . . .

Featherstonhaugh blinked hard at an incipient headache. He removed the spectacles and rubbed his eyes. When he opened them, his vision was doubled. Two identical sets of bones, one belonging to an elephant and one to a mastodon, were superimposed upon one another.

He blinked again. His eyes began to focus properly, as though a film had been removed. Hays still held the bones, but they were only that: the bones of a long-dead creature, shattered and incomplete. They told a story to those who knew how to look at them, but not nearly so interesting or vibrant a story as the one he had just seen.

He folded the spectacles closed and placed them on the table. Though dizzy, he did not fall.

Hays watched him with evident concern, but Featherstonhaugh was not prepared to assume the other man had his best interests at heart. "The right side of the head is, indeed, beautifully preserved." There was a tremor in his voice. He swallowed and the action or the pause proved helpful.

Hays set the bones down once more. "Do you wish to continue your examination?"

Featherstonhaugh followed the other man's gaze, not to the bones but to the spectacles. He had the inkling that Hays cared little for his opinions of the ancient animal. "No, thank you." His voice was steadier, at least. "Having seen the specimen, I will look at others to compare. Perhaps I will return later."

"Viewing evidence with fresh eyes is valuable," Hays said.

With an effort, Featherstonhaugh refrained from shuddering and beat a passably dignified retreat. He kept one hand on the curving banister. He was lightheaded, as though untethered. He feared that he might slip and smash open his skull, or that he might float away entirely.

Hays, chatting politely, seemed infinitely more embedded—in his body, in this city, in this reality. It was a preposterous illusion, of course. Featherstonhaugh was no less real than the man beside him. And though he had been born across the ocean, though his family was not part of Philadelphia society, though he was only part of New York society by virtue of his marriage, he had no less right to occupy this place than Hays.

And yet it was Hays who remained within Philosophical Hall, and Featherstonhaugh who walked away.

The State House clock showed how little time had passed, how little time was necessary to shake the foundations of one's world. But the clock also served as a reminder of its maker, Lukens, and his crusade against Redheffer's spurious perpetual motion machine. It had taken time and effort for Lukens to build a machine that proved Redheffer's a fraud, but prove it he did, and in this very city.

Featherstonhaugh took a steadying breath. He did not know what Hays had done—yet. But he had some guesses as to why he had done it. The cliques of Philadelphia's intellectual community were well-known, and those alliances could be stronger than the allegiance to truth which every man of science ought to hold dear. Misguided loyalty was bad enough; engaging in fraud was far less forgivable. Featherstonhaugh was not by nature a particularly forgiving man, and he had no intention of letting Hays win the game he played.

It was not merely an affront to natural history, but to Featherstonhaugh personally. To conjure forth a nonexistent creature, to suggest that it had walked the same hillsides as Featherstonaugh himself . . . The image was, suddenly, quite unbearable. He could almost feel the erasure of some essential, if hitherto unknown, aspect of his old estate. A juvenile mastodon, that was right and proper. That belonged to the far-distant past of the place where he had raised children and imported the best agricultural products.

Featherstonhaugh meant to prove that elephants had never meandered across his old estate, or any other part of the continent. The days of *Tetracauldodon mastodontoideum* were numbered. He was a geologist, well-positioned to argue the truth of the matter.

As he walked, his determination and confidence grew. He had no destination in mind, but took great comfort from the cobblestones beneath his feet. No matter what he had seen—or thought he had seen, or been forced to see—the stones were real. The very bones of the continent were real, and he meant to understand their true shape.

The Time Traveler's Assistant Discovers What Could Have Been

~ *Scott Edelman*

The Time Traveler's Assistant, understanding that whether the Time Traveler himself spent many months or mere moments in the past correlated not at all to the speed with which the world moved forward in this present, this future, expected the universe to instantaneously change by the time the blinding flash signaling the world's first successful human transmission faded.

The control room's barely functional equipment, with lights which often threw off sparks as they blinked data updates; the log book going back decades, tracking the far too many deaths caused by their experiments; the off-putting portrait fading with the years as it hung askew on one wall, keeping the target of their project constantly in their minds; even the flavor of the air, not yet fully recovered from all the wars between then and now, and perhaps never to do so without their intervention . . . each of these things and many more should have altered. But they had not.

To their great frustration, the Time Traveler's Assistant noted—alone now in a room where moments before there had been two—everything was as it had been.

Did that mean the mission had failed?

Perhaps. But perhaps it had succeeded.

Or perhaps both. That was one way the time streams could be perceived, at least according to certain of the physicists.

But the Time Traveler's Assistant believed in the actual, not the theoretical, such was their training, and so, as minutes passed, with nothing in the room having transformed, they knew—someone would have to follow.

And looking at the dials beneath their fingers they then knew—*they* would have to follow. And not years from now. But *now* now.

The Time Traveler's Assistant had not anticipated this.

The Time Traveler's Assistant did not want this.

But unexpectedly, enough energy remained pulsing through the interconnected machinery which filled the squalid warehouse to allow for one more trip. The group—impatient as only those attempting time travel could be—would not have to wait years for a second attempt.

And there was no time to tell the others, because it needed to happen before the power faded, or else this precious opportunity to possibly prevent yesterday's catastrophe would be lost. They flipped the switches once more, exactly as they had mere moments before, only this time, as the small, dark room began to echo with a hum which grew into an urgent crackle, the Time Traveler's Assistant without hesitation stepped from behind the control board and into the blindingly bright chamber.

So brilliant was the room they could barely make out the nearby door fly open, and so loud they could not decipher the shouts. But it did not matter. There was no time to explain their sudden need to disappear.

And then the blaze of white nothing vanished, and as the eyes of the Time Traveler's Assistant adjusted, they could see the walls which had surrounded them had vanished as well, and they were standing in only rubble and ash, bent rebar and broken bricks, without a sense of having travelled. It was almost as if the room which had been about them had abruptly collapsed. But not quite . . . for not even the footprint of their former boundaries was there any longer.

They were now . . . elsewhere.

They had done it after all. They had gone back. But . . . to where?

The coordinates the team had carefully calculated should not have taken the Time Traveler who'd preceded them to a place of such devastation, and the Time Traveler's Assistant—who briefly thought they perhaps no longer needed to think of themselves as merely an Assistant, for they were now a Time Traveler as well—knew they shouldn't have arrived in the midst of such destruction either, for the sealed fate they were hoping to avert still waited in the (now) future place between their own (left behind) future and this (present) past.

They stood ankle deep in red ash, beside a brick wall which had collapsed just enough to create a ledge low enough to peer over. The air was both fouler and purer than what they exhaled from their own time in the moments after their arrival, a paradox they set aside to contemplate later. But for now . . . where was now? Were they inside of what was once a building? Or outside? There was no clear way to tell. But they could hear voices, and until they were able to determine whether those belonged to people who might try to stop them from accomplishing their mission, it was best to stay hidden, even though . . .

What was their mission anyway? The Time Traveler had one, and had the training to see it through, but that was then and this was now—or maybe it was also then, for time was a confusing thing—and there was no way, based on their environment, that the same task as previously devised could possibly cure the ills they'd inherited.

They looked over the barrier and saw the identical red dust in which they stood stretched all the way to the horizon, punctuated by rubble, and as well as dozens of people who were walking about, apparently aimlessly, leaving trails of mist rising in their wakes. Remarkably for all the stirring up of the grit of what had been lost, the air did not smell of destruction—which they continued to find surprising. It was a better scent than that of the world left behind, and with its unfamiliar tang, almost pleasant.

Someone coughed to their side, far too close for comfort in this or any age. They took a sudden step away and fell back over a brick, a cloud of dust rising to swallow not only them but also the one who had approached.

As the particles settled around them, the Time Traveler's Assistant looked up at what presented as a woman according to their memories of the signifiers of this time. They were glad for the dust which had coated their garb, for it would perhaps mean they would not seem as out of place as they felt. After all, there had been no way to prepare for a journey the way the Time Traveler had. And the cougher's hard-worn clothing was years old, as was their own, but unlike their own, her multi-layered clothing was ragged and filthy. She made no notice of that distinction between them, though, seemed concerned only with a photograph in her outstretched hand.

"I'm sorry," she said, with a cracked voice which spoke of an age even greater than she seemed under the grime. "Please forgive me. I didn't mean to startle you. But have you seen my husband? They took him away. They—"

Her voice cracked, and she lowered her head, pushing the photograph closer.

The Time Traveler's Assistant thought the photo so blurry, the image could have been of anyone, perhaps even the Time Traveler himself—was that why the machine had brought them back to this time and place?—because there was a fix which required them to both take action at once?—but then blinked to clear the tears and grit from their eyes, and saw . . . no. So they shook their head, to which the woman said no more, only backed slowly away, mumbling, then turned to vanish around the other side of the wall.

The Time Traveler's Assistant got back to their feet and peered carefully around the wall's edge, watching as the woman hobbled into the distance. But as she vanished, they rose fully, for what was the point in hiding? The team hadn't been working to wash away the centuries only to waste the moments which were then revealed.

Dozens of people milled about in what could have been mistaken for a vast desert, if not for the wreckage scattered about. Perhaps one of them might be made to reveal information which would explain what had pulled them to this date and time. But whom to approach first?

They came out from behind their hiding place, entered the orbit of bodies, and moved slowly about within them. Some seemed familiar with the path they trod, and cloaked in regret, while others picked their way slowly forward as if all was new to them. Surveying the faces of these long dead, they struggled to remember the lessons of this time, such as how to greet in a non-threatening way, how to ask without seeming overly inquisitive, how to move one's body without giving offense, all lessons the original Time Traveler had so well memorized—until they came upon what at first appeared to be a mound of discarded cloth.

They paused for a moment, for such scraps seemed odd to be abandoned in that way, considering the threadbare condition of those who moved nearby, to whom such shreds would surely be precious—and to their great surprise realized . . . no. There was movement beneath the rags. There was . . . a body.

They knelt and folded back a patchwork of rough cloth to find . . . a child.

It had been a long while since the Time Traveler's Assistant had seen anybody so young, one of the many crises the Time Traveler's trip back was meant to solve, and yet, but a symptom of the true crisis.

"Are you all right, child?" they asked. "Is anyone taking care of you?"

It was a question the Time Traveler's Assistant almost did not bother asking, for so self-absorbed were each of those around them it was an answer in itself. Whatever this place once might have been, it was no longer a community. It had been shattered. Shattered by the one they would centuries hence band together to stop.

The child curled up more deeply within its cloth, and frantically backed away, heels etching ruts into the red dust beneath.

"No," they continued. "Don't be afraid. I'm not here to harm you. There's no need to be afraid of me."

"It's not you he's afraid of. It's all of us. It's everyone."

The Time Traveler's Assistant turned to see a young man, or what appeared to be a young man. This moment demanded judgement which they, up in their own era, did not have to make. Why did things in the past have to be so complicated? A slash of cloth across his face obscured one eye.

In response to their obvious gaze, he pointed toward his face, then held his arms wide to encompass everything about him.

"That was what came from trying to prevent this," he said.

"Are you . . . ?" They were afraid to say the words, for fear they could be true. What could he have meant by prevention? Could he be yet another time traveler, a later follower who leapt back years after them, once the team regrouped and was able to make a further attempt to change what the Time Traveler had not, and what they themselves had not yet changed, would not change?

"Yes," he said, though the words which followed proved his answer to what was in their thoughts was actually no. "I am. And I'm not the only protester nearly killed by a supposedly non-lethal pellet. Non-lethal? What's that supposed to mean? There's nothing that isn't lethal, not when used by people like *them*. I'm lucky an eye was all I lost. It could have been worse. Much worse. At least my cracked skull healed."

He rapped the top of his head with his knuckles and smiled.

The Time Traveler's Assistant swallowed, not ready for this world, not knowing what they were being called on to do, if in fact anything could be done.

"And the child?"

They looked over at the mound beneath where the wriggling had stopped ever since the Time Traveler's Assistant had ceased addressing it.

"I've never heard him speak," answered the man. "At least—not words. All I know is, he was once taken from his parents and caged, because of . . ."

He voice trailed off, and he pressed his lips tightly together. Instead of continuing, he merely shrugged, as if to say—there was, of course, no *need* to say. Was there?

"Ever since then, those of us who are able, watch out for him as best we can, give him food, offer shelter when the storms come. He doesn't always accept it. He's broken."

"That is kind of you."

"Well," he said, shrugging again, and looking at the invisible child. "We're all broken. So tell me—where have you come from?"

Before the Time Traveler's Assistant could answer, could even begin to think of how to answer—because though the Time Traveler had rehearsed believable identities, plausible histories, they had done no such thing—another voice behind joined the questioning, only this one was loud and angry.

"Yes, where do you come from? I haven't seen you here before. Why are you here?"

The Time Traveler's Assistant turned and froze at the sight of the large man, never having been questioned in such a manner. He tugged at his grimy red cap, so shredded there was barely enough band left to the thing to hold the brim in place, and spat at their feet.

"We don't get strangers around here often, and when we do, we don't like them. And not just that—what religion are you? Huh? What's wrong with you? Why aren't you saying anything? Come on, tell me—where do you come from?"

Before they could give any answer at all, not a word, not even a syllable, her assailant moved even closer, and shouted.

"Forget it! Don't bother answering! I don't give a damn. It doesn't matter. Wherever it was, why don't you go back where you came from?"

The Time Traveler's Assistant surprised themselves by emitting a sob which vibrated their entire body so deeply their knees almost buckled, because the question brought home what they already knew, but had been trying to keep the recognition of at a distance. Go back where they came from? They could not. They could never return to where they'd been mere minutes before. This was a one-way trip, just as it had been for the Time Traveler who'd preceded them. And not just because no such mechanism to boomerang home existed—but because the loss of home was the entire point of such a trip. Where they came from, if all was successful, should no longer exist.

"Back off," said the one-eyed man to the hate-filled newcomer, interposing himself between them. "Your old wars have no place here. Leave the visitor alone."

"Why don't you mind your own business?" came the reply, along with a push, and then the two of them were rolling in the dust. The Time Traveler's Assistant could barely make them out beneath the rising red mist.

They took that moment, after one last look at the pile of cloth beneath which hid a broken child, to move on. But there seemed to be nowhere to move on *to*, no possible point of purpose. All that was around were the ruins of what once was—distressing evidence of what the initial Time Traveler had been sent to the past to prevent. Yes, they supposed a society of sorts had grown out of the wreckage between the past and their present, now future, but the centuries of pain between those two points seemed insurmountable. So much had been lost, so much seemed beyond recovery.

Faced with the reality of what once had been theoretical, it was impossible to deny that The Time Traveler had failed. And because of the endless dust and ash which stretched far into the distance, masking any horizon, the Time Traveler's Assistant knew they would not succeed. But neither would they fail. They hadn't even been given a chance to try.

They were too late. What had happened had already happened, and it would be up to another to fix what was for them clearly unfixable.

They walked away, trying to ignore the shouting of the men behind, and the whimpering of the child as well. Each brought on a great despair at being able to communicate with anyone here. Perhaps this meant communication outside one's own time wasn't possible. Shuffling ahead, though, they knew they had to try.

In the middle distance, they could make out a waist-high rectangular block built of bricks and wood, behind which sat a man. Or what seemed at first glance to be a man, for the true details of the figure were masked beneath a conglomeration of strange artifacts with which he'd adorned himself.

His face had been smeared with what appeared to be clay, and atop his head were twigs woven together to form a helmet of sorts, almost as if what once was hair had solidified. As the Time Traveler's Assistant drew closer, they understood the construction before the man to be a crude desk he had made for himself. He pushed papers across the surface, occasionally slashing at one with the point of a small, broken stick, appearing to act out some type of signing ritual.

There was something far too familiar about the man, impossibly familiar, and as the Time Traveler's Assistant approached even nearer, a fading portrait popped into their memory, one seen so often as to have become little more than the background noise of their former life. They froze. Their feet became lead, and after a beat, they almost backed away.

Almost.

As they quivered in that moment of indecision, the man looked up, noticing them. He smiled, his teeth bizarrely white against that discolored face, and waved them over with fingers too small for the hand which bore them.

The Time Traveler's Assistant stood before the makeshift desk, trying to see this man as he had been before, stripping him of mud, and twigs, and the immeasurable weight of crushed history. And seeing what was revealed, they thought. . .this cannot be. They must be mistaken. They could not have been randomly brought to this here, this now, this . . . this man.

And then he flung open his arms, taking in the ground on which they stood, and all the horrors which ringed them, and said, "I alone can fix this."

Only then was the Time Travelers's Assistant certain that . . . yes.

Yes, they thought. Yes. *But—*

"No," they said. "No, you can't. It's far too late for that."

"What did you say?" asked the man, anger in his voice. They could tell he was unused to being contradicted. They *knew* he was unused to being contradicted, one of the reasons time travel was the only way to repair the future.

It was too late to fix what had been broken, perhaps. But not too late for justice. The Time Traveler's Assistant reached across the mockery of a desk, and by the overly long strip of cloth which hung from his neck, grabbed the man, the one whose incompetence, arrogance, ignorance, and greed had caused all this. That he had survived what he had wrought was an abomination. They began to pull him across the top of the structure he had built. They would take care of this man, and then dismantle the replica of a desk he never deserved to have.

"Hey!" he shouted, as his helmet flew off and vanished into the dust. "Hey, hey, hey! You can't do that."

The man's voice changed then with his protestations, in tone, in timber, no longer embodying the bluster of before, and as the Time Traveler's Assistant pulled him along, toward the wall behind which they had first manifested, he started to shout nonsense words, seeming to speak not just to them, but to the universe. They could not understand the man's meaning, but assumed the words would have made sense if they'd shared the same time of birth. No matter—once they were out of sight of the others, the two of them would talk, and the Time Traveler's Assistant would make him understand what he had done. If he was capable of understanding, that is.

But before they had gone more than a few meters, the Time Traveler's Assistant was tackled and separated from their captive. They were surprised to see their assailants were the two men who'd earlier been fighting—each now held one of their arms, no longer appearing to be enemies—and even the comatose child, suddenly energetic, had joined the group, pushing at their back.

A few more joined them to make sure the Time Traveler's Assistant had no choice but to walk where they pulled, and as others rushed forward to hold electronic devices in their direction, they were dragged toward what at first seemed a far distant horizon, but once through a wall of smoke and fog, was revealed to be something more, a flaw in their previous perception. The land did not continue on the other side, for there was only a wall, one painted to resemble a dwindling continuation of what had been left behind. Then a door opened, and they moved through it to a room bare of destruction.

The Time Traveler's Assistant was startled to see people there with crisp clothes and clean faces, and machinery, too, not so very different in appearance from what had sent them from far in the future, and numerous small screens on which could be seen the land of red dust they'd just left behind. So many questions filled their mind, but before they could utter any of them, they were hustled through another door, one which brought them outside again, only this outside, a true outside, was nothing like the former outside—a false outside, the Time Traveler's Assistant now understood—from which they'd been banished.

Before they could take it all in, they were spun about. Only one other remained with them. It was her defender, the one missing an eye, who removed the cloth from across his face to reveal—that was another illusion. Unlike his earlier welcoming demeanor, he was angry now, and no longer willing to take their side.

"I don't know what that was all about, but you're out of here. I don't even know how you got in. Everybody on the list is accounted for, and you're not one of them. You didn't have a ticket."

The Time Traveler's Assistant said nothing, far more disoriented by the journey they'd taken over the past minute than they'd been by the one which had encompassed centuries.

"Why would you want to sneak in?" he continued. "Why would you want to ruin everything for everybody? Keep moving, and we won't have to get the police involved."

He waited for an answer, then frowned, and turned, and went back through the doors from which they'd both come.

As he vanished, they gawked at the building in front of them, and at the sign above the door through which they'd just been pushed. A marquee read:

WHAT COULD HAVE BEEN

And beneath that, in slightly smaller letters:

AN IMMERSIVE EXPERIENCE
OF A FUTURE THAT NEVER WAS

Below those large letters, between two doors which led to the mock world from which they'd been evicted, was a poster illustrated with a grotesque drawing of the man the Time Traveler had previously gone back to prevent from being born, and wrapping round that image a barely decipherable—to their eyes—script which told them of the lie they'd just been living:

> *Experience the tomorrow which was almost ours in a fully interactive experience. Freely wander the world from which we were rescued, and be grateful. Six performances only.*

The Time Traveler's Assistant understood now. They'd arrived at a where and when unattached to any change point they could manipulate to save their future, and the man they thought deserved punishment was not at all that man, only some sort of actor. But if that were so, then . . . where was now? They'd felt lost earlier attempting to unravel the meaning of the world of red dust, the world which proved to be an illusion, but felt no less lost now that a truth had been revealed. Was this what the Time Traveler himself had experienced on his failed mission? Had he become lost as well, first in time, and then to despair?

They dropped to the curb, devoid of a desire to go on, and took several gulps of the fresh air—fresher than the remembered world of the future left behind, and fresher by far than the false future from which they'd just been evicted—hoping to clear their mind. They slapped red dust off their jacket, and when the flecks settled, took another deep breath, and for the first time, truly looked at this outer world into which they'd been thrust.

The structures around them stood tall, nothing like the false future in the building behind, or the middle future which waited between the past as the Time Traveler's Assistant understood it and the future they'd left behind. The casualness of those who wandered nearby was almost infuriating, for they felt the people who walked down the street should be celebrating. Shouldn't they? How could they be oblivious to the absence of the horrible days ahead which had somehow been lifted from them?

Or would it have been their present? There was no way of knowing. For this time was most definitely not the time it was supposed to be, and instead one in which the destruction caused by a madman had been transmuted from reality into a theatrical performance, so perhaps the Time Traveler who proceeded them had caused a change after all. But if so, then why was the world the Time Traveler's Assistant had left behind unchanged? Why had they needed to follow into that blazing chamber?

A hum arose from behind as if in answer to their questions, and when they turned toward the all-too-familiar sound, they saw the theater which had fooled them was gone, and in its place, a flickering circle, close enough and large enough so the world behind was subsumed in a crackling of energy which grew into a wall of lightning struggling to coalesce into something more. They instinctively recoiled, throwing an arm over their eyes.

Once the brightness dimmed and they could bear to look again, they saw the coruscating sparks had become a shimmering window, and on the other side stood those with whom the Time Traveler's Assistant had until that afternoon worked, only . . . older. *Much* older.

The room her friends occupied was an unfamiliar one, too, with equipment even more complicated than that which had propelled them there. They recognized the woman at the center of the group as someone who had once been her peer, though based on her position in the room, and the deferential glances of the others, was now the leader. Her eyes widened on seeing them, but though she moved her lips, no sound came.

The Time Traveler's Assistant shook their head, and spoke, to which their old friend—now truly old—also shook her head, then frowned. She twisted a screen to face out through the portal, then looked down and began typing.

"It is good to see you again after all these years," scrolled the words.

"It is good to see you as well," said the Time Traveler's Assistant, then fell silent, not merely because they knew they could not be heard, but due to the sight of their friend's tears rolling down through what the years had made of her. They thought of how their own brief moment had turned into their comrade's decades, and how the gaps each had experienced could not possibly be compared.

"We have good news," the scrolling went on. "We located a message the first traveler had left behind for us, etched into metal plates and buried where he knew we would find them, which meant that once we finally perfected the technology, we were able to pinpoint that time of fracture between when you and your predecessor landed, and thus able to complete the original mission. Actually, no. Not quite the original mission, but one close enough so the things which were meant to happen did not. The world he was sent back to prevent was never born. The path you followed in hopes of changing no longer needs to be changed. We have taken a step sideways, breaking free of that time stream. And you have shuffled sideways as well."

Their friend looked up from the keyboard then, a radiant expression evident on her face. But that faded as soon as their eyes met, and she returned to her typing.

"Oh, how I wish you could see it. How I wish we could bring you back to learn what we have become. But . . . we haven't perfected the means of return, and don't know if we ever will. We wanted you to know, though . . . to know we have done as we hoped. We have to go now. There isn't enough power to continue this transmission. We are sorry."

The Time Traveler's Assistant's friend looked up one final time, and nodded. They nodded, too. Silently, they tried in every physical way they knew how to make sure those left behind understood they were accepting of their fate.

They would have to be.

The portal shrunk away until, with a final pop and a metallic smell, it vanished, revealing the building behind and the theater's front door. The Time Traveler's Assistant stepped inside, and behind a counter saw one of the men who'd only watched as they'd been dragged by before being tossed out.

"I am sorry," they said to him. "May I go back? I promise I won't cause any more trouble. I . . . I understand now."

He looked at them for a few moments, expression blank, and the Time Traveler's Assistant was about to continue their pleading when he nodded, then led them to a doorway. Once opened, the Time Traveler's Assistant looked through on the future which never happened, populated with actors who only pretended to suffer the fates the election of a madman would cause, and in the distance, the actor who pretended to be that man himself.

"What could have been," they whispered.

"Yes," said man beside them. "That's the name of the show. Are you going in?"

The Time Traveler's Assistant stood silently for one further moment, looking at the past they in a small way had helped prevent, and then stepped through, joyfully kicking up the dust of a future which never was.

Culture of Silence

~ W. T. Paterson

The bone broth simmered on the stove as the text from my sister Luna came through. *He hit me, Riley. Again. Broke the necklace.* I turned off the burner and opened the cupboard beneath the sink. Two packed duffle bags ready, our contingency plan, an escape route that never felt like a plan B, but rather something inevitable. We'd meet halfway in the Ozarks if I couldn't talk her down, a cabin tucked deep in the woods away from my New England residence, and far from her adopted Christian, West Texas town.

Breathe, I wrote back. *Suppress the urge to unleash.*

Of course he hit her, the bastard of a husband had no idea, and weak men had an unyielding need to feel strong by attacking those who showed kindness. The weak have a certain self-proclaimed entitlement to fury endowed by their perceived laws of nature. A local Christian radio host with ten thousand daily listeners, my sister's husband Gabe had a following that would blindly side with him should she ever come forward with allegations. That's what scared me the most.

Outside, the day had maybe an hour of sunlight left before the autumn moon declared victory over the sky and I
was no stranger to how the full moon brought out the worst
in the world. Neighborhood cats mewled under porch
steps with deep, guttural warnings. Dogs paced fenced-in
yards with hair spiked down their spine. Treebound birds
sang in furious prose only to fall as silent as a tomb.

People were no better. They drove like maniac heathens
swerving between lanes, jamming on brakes, attempting
to break the sound barrier with howling engines, and got
into confrontations with total strangers over the most
peculiar things. That morning, a neighbor had knocked
on my door demanding that the stench from my basement be dealt with.

"Smelting," I told the short, squat man. "A lost art."

"Whatever it is, it stinks," the man said. He thrust his
arms and balled hands by his side like a toddler throwing
a tantrum.

An old New England house with a stone and dirt basement, the previous owners were a family of jewelers from
the 1800's and had left behind their kiln, lead pans, and
scales. Even though I used an exhaust fan modified into
a dryer vent that connected to the furnace chimney, that
heavy wet-dog scent fell back toward the earth like a
cursed soul instead of up against the heavens into saint-
hood. I bought, sold, restored, and designed silver jewelry, same as my father.

"I'll see what I can do," I said, pinching my eyes. I
reached into my pocket and pulled out a thin silver

bracelet. "Take this. As an apology. Made it myself."

The neighbor collected the bracelet in his palm with a side smirk.

"A man ain't supposed to give another man jewelry 'les they . . . you know. You one of them?"

"One of what?" I asked. I knew what the neighbor implied, weak men love to attempt emasculation, but they also crumbled under scrutiny. Watching him squirm held a certain satisfaction.

"It's jus' I ain't seen women comin' and goin'," he said.

"Then I'm like you," I said, and the man's bald head went as red as the leaves on the autumnal trees. "Single. Nasty divorce."

What weak men don't realize is that if you back someone into a corner that knows how to fight, they better take note of their exits. The divorce part wasn't true, but true enough in that it shut the man up. After what happened with my parents, I doubted I'd ever get married.

My neighbor pocketed the bracelet and nodded his way down the steps.

Now as the sun set, I watched him through a window gather with his male friends around a firepit. Their guts pushed against their shirts as round as the moon, bottles of beer in hand, single malt whiskey being passed around, howling with laughter like the faux dog-men they were.

I'm done, Luna wrote. If there was an hour of daylight here, that meant she had two before a cover of darkness might better hide the damage.

What happened? I asked, not to uncover the source and imply that she might be somewhat to blame, but to bide time. If I could get her talking, I could cool her rabid heart.

He. Hit. Me. I'm done with this culture of silence. I speak up, they'll say I deserved it and call me a bitch. I stay quiet, he thinks he's right to do it again.

She got it from my mother, likened herself after the woman, that hot and cold polarity of emotion. Catch her right and she was the kindest, most loyal person on the planet. Cross her or her pups and she'd change into something unholy that made entire neighborhoods cower in fear.

One time, a boy pushed my sister down the twisty slide at the playground. She tumbled across the plastic bends as static shocks nipped at her exposed flesh. My mother leapt to her feet and grabbed the boy by the back of his neck demanding to know where his parents were. The kid pointed to a bench where a guy in untied boots and dirty jeans sipped from a paper bag. She marched over and gave the man the what-for so bad that he collected his son and booked it.

"Sometimes, you gotta show the world you have teeth," our mother told us. We walked home under the canopy of fiery red leaves. It wasn't the worst I'd ever seen her lash out, those times when our father packed us into a car to get away were once in a blue moon, but our mother's sense of justice was a beast in and of itself. My sister had that same thing, that gene that made her snap and change into something feral. Only no one ever saw it really come out because it never had to. Our father was the counterbalance to add perspective because once home, the police showed up to ask questions. They brought my mother to the station.

"But that boy pushed ME," my sister pleaded with my dad, her sad puppy-dog eyes brown and full.

"I know," he sighed. "But when a woman shows the world she has teeth, scared men try to pull them from her mouth. There's nothing more dangerous than scared men in power."

Later, my mother came home. No charges pressed, but my parents argued with their door closed until the small hours of the morning. The next night, my mother wore a brand-new necklace that my father crafted. She needed to feel loved, and jewelry was her love language. It was like she was a different person with that necklace, calm to the stressors of life and care-free. Whatever had been brewing inside of her had been pacified with that necklace. It had been silenced. We never really spoke about it again.

And that boy and his father never once gave us any more trouble beyond hushed whispers in line at the grocer.

Sometimes silence has teeth of its own.

The men next door built their fire too large and gawked at the reaching flame. Their need to destroy and dominate the inanimate spoke to a deep-seeded insecurity of a time that could have been, never was, or falsely yet to come.

Bags are packed, I wrote. *You say the word.*

Fuck the bags, she wrote, and my heart thumped with dread. She meant business and inside of that small, Christian, West Texas town, there'd be hell to pay if she wasn't careful.

But I guess that was kind of her point.

You don't have to do anything, I wrote. *Just leave.*

You sound scared, she wrote. *Stay quiet, no retribution, move on and pretend it's all ok.*

That's not what I meant, and you know it, I wrote.

The night stalked forward swallowing the edges of daylight in its mighty teeth. The laughter of the men next door sounded like wild animals gathered around a carcass jawing and snapping at meaty bones. I pulled open the cupboard with my knee and looked at the packed duffle bags. I'd leave if I had to, but I really didn't want to. After moving so much as kids, this two-story New England house finally had the feel of home, a place where Mom and Dad could visit and be proud.

If they ever came out of hiding, of course.

When my sister told me she'd met someone, I had natural reservations. Not just as a big brother, but real reservations about who this guy pretended to be. Outgoing, polished, and magnetic, he knew how to draw and maintain crowds. That radio voice was the salve to soothe the burns of the exhausted working class, but underneath was a small, terrified boy hiding in the shadows of the man he had become. It was something about the way he interacted with people and bullied them away under the guise of being helpful. Never fully present, never spending too much time with any one person, it was like he was afraid of anyone seeing the real him.

"So, Texas," I said the first time we met. At a barbecue cooking salmon, chicken wings, and ribs, I stood next to the grill watching my sister catch the scent of cooking meats in her nose. Summer food made her the happiest. Gabe smiled his toothy grin and pushed a hand through his salon-quality hair.

"You know what they say about Texas," he said and winked.

"What do they say?" I asked. I flipped the wings and ribs to let the sizzle of the fat roar like applause from a ballgame.

"You know," he said and winked again. He nudged me with his elbow. "Everything's bigger . . . doesn't matter. Hey, would you mind getting me a fresh brew? One more sip and this bottle is dead."

He put a hand on my shoulder and squeezed, then pointed to the plastic tub with ice and bottles along the fence in the backyard. I pulled down the grill cover and went to get him a drink. By the time I came back, he asked if the food was ready.

Luna met him at a charity event, one of those minor league baseball nights where a cut of the gate went to wildlife preservation. She got selected from the crowd to play the line drive challenge where people stood in the outfield as professional batters nailed balls toward the fence. Whoever caught the most won $100, plus a special shoutout in the charity's monthly newsletter.

Luna loved minor league ballgames. The crack of the bat, the fast pitches, the constant game of catch, she was in her element near the field. When her name got pulled, she hustled to the bathroom to pee before making her way out onto the stretch of green.

The first two contestants didn't catch anything. They both high tailed it from center field, to right, to left. The third got lucky and caught a looping fly ball, but when Luna took to the grass and loaded up on her haunches, she watched the batters and their fly balls with an almost obsessive focus. She caught every single line drive and I sat back thinking the jig was up.

Gabe, impressed by her performance, introduced himself and explained his status in that Christian, West Texas town before asking her on a date.

"You sure?" I asked her later that night after she explained how she had a good feeling about this one. Luna smiled and nodded.

"Everyone has a role, everyone has a place," she said. Christian towns tended to let outsiders know real quick if they were welcome or not. Most often, they silently demanded that a person play their expected part and not deviate. Something about a man's role and a woman's place, a mindset stuck in a bygone era.

"And if he expects you to just . . . obey?" I asked.

"It can be satisfying knowing what someone wants, and then giving it to them," Luna said, and I could see in her face that she'd made up her mind.

That night, I packed the plan B bags just to be safe.

Outside, the men around the fire pointed to the ground-level windows of my basement. My neighbor seemed to be explaining to them about the silver and gold I kept down there for smelting. He held up the bracelet and made an obscene, airy gesture with his hand and pranced around in a circle. His buddies laughed, but one of them asked to see the bracelet.

"It's yours," my neighbor said, and his friend slid the bracelet on. He admired it in the flickering light of the fire. The irony seemed lost on my neighbor.

The first time Gabe hit my sister, she told me at a local flea market while we waded through the aisles looking for trinkets and treasures. The sun-bleached wooden tables threatened splinters to the unaware. Vendors puffed at cigarettes and barked with promises that all prices were negotiable.

"Leave him," I said. She'd come to visit for a week to let the dust settle.

"I can't," she said. "The community would hate me."

"Who cares?" I said. I bent over and picked up an old pocket watch. It had stopped at 11:58. Two minutes to midnight, or midday.

"That's $30," the vendor said, an older woman with wrinkles so deep that they cast their own shadows.

"For tin?" I asked.

"That's copper," the woman said. I looked at the watch again. It wasn't copper. It still maintained its shine, even though the date etched into the back read 1920.

"Copper oxidizes and turns green. Tin doesn't. This is tin," I said and put it back on the table. The woman picked up the watch and held it close to her eyes, then called out for her husband to come take a look. The tone in her voice lilted with betrayal.

"You're so good at seeing things for what they are," Luna said.

"Leave him," I said again, and Luna pawed at me like I was playing.

"Let's not talk about it anymore," she said, and shoved everything down to that dark place inside of her that collected pain and guilt, that dark inner kiln that altered the physical makeup of everything locked within.

I should have listened, Luna wrote. *Especially after what happened with Mom.*

You're not Mom, I wrote.

She passed on the bitch, Luna wrote.

Our parents left in the night when I was twenty and Luna was seventeen. Our mother had fallen into one of her moods after a drunk man assaulted her and the cops passed it off by saying the attacker was just drunk and fooling around, to let it go, that he never intended to hurt her. My mother's bruised wrist and swollen cheek told a different story.

My father packed their stuff. He said we'd understand one day, that my sister and I needed to leave this place at dawn and change our names, but to not go outside before then, that it was my job to look after Luna. Though we followed his commands and sloshed through the bleeding streets lined with limbs at sunup, the pain of abandonment never healed.

When Luna left for Texas, I thought she'd be able to handle herself. I gave her a silver necklace fashioned from our mother's old jewelry to double down, to let her know I cared. Love languages and such.

But with the necklace broken and tensions rising like the fur on a dog's back, I felt only failure.

Call me, I wrote. My phone buzzed and I answered halfway through the first ring.

"I'm sorry to drag you into this," Luna said, and my heart dropped.

"Be better than her," I whispered, and through the receiver Luna whimpered.

"Weak men . . ." she said. "I'll see you at the cabin."

Over the phone, I heard the tearing of flesh and painful cries of a body in transformation. Luna grunted and coughed as I imagined thick fur tearing through tender skin. Outside, the darkness had settled, and the full moon stood victorious in the dark sky. Shadows had already begun to fall over that Christian, West Texas town that would never see morning. I heard panting, then the gruesome snapping of jaws.

She was her mother's daughter alright.

As the call went dead, the men next door howled. They peeled off their shirts and swung them like helicopter blades above their heads, their back hair and chest hair patchy and thinning. Whatever they thought they were, they weren't.

I grabbed the bags and dumped the bone broth down the sink. Steam rose and fogged the windows creating momentary privacy as I killed the lights, said goodbye to the house that had finally begun feeling like home, and escaped through the front door.

That culture of silence works both ways.

Along the twisting backroads of my small New England town, the moon pierced the tips of the trees to create shadows in the forest where, if I squinted and looked away, I could vaguely make out the shape of my mother and father waving goodbye.

The Thawing of Rev. Jules LeRoux

~ Ben Curl

*THE TRANSFORMATION OF REV. JULES LEROUX.
1ST STAGE—SATURDAY, OCTOBER 15, 1870. DEER
LAKE. WHERE I STEP INTO THE WATERS. FROM
WHENCE I SHALL NOT RETURN UNTIL THE
THAW. STRIPPED OF THIS WEARIED FLESH, YET
YOU SHALL NOT FIND THESE BRITTLE BONES.
YOU WILL FIND ME AS I AM, AS I WAS, AS I
WASN'T MEANT TO BE BUT NEVERTHELESS AM
AND AM FREE. COME ONE, COME ALL, TO WIT-
NESS WHAT WILL BE BORN OF ICE.*

When she plucked the crumpled flyer from the pocket
of my trousers, mother sat me down on the wobbly stool
papa had carved for me. With her finger on my chin, she
bent my neck at a harsh angle to look her in the eyes.

"You shouldn't be listening to him."

"I'm not. I swear I'm not, mother."

But I was.

Nothing in this world could stop me from listening.

The stooped figure and rambling words of Reverend
LeRoux had insinuated themselves into my daily existence. He was the soft winter wind outside my window
at night.

In a past life, I was a bird, a rare bluebird. From the gutters I spewed seeds and the insides of worms, into the mouths of young who were not my own, who had been abandoned by their wayward parents. From the alleyways I rescued stray cats, leading them to a purpose, a common cause. Because of these sacrileges, the townsfolk would not forgive me.

"Why were they angry?" I asked. "You didn't do anything wrong."

Don't listen to what they tell you of right and wrong. He was sitting on an overturned tree stump, outside the edge of a pile of waste rock, stooping lower and lower into the setting sun. His shoulders were as low as the top of the stump. *Those aren't the things they'll kill you for.*

"Do you mean that they killed you? Back when you were a bluebird, I mean?"

My memory of those times is hazy. But, yes. He shook his hide, sending a spray of twigs and dried leaves from his back. *I believe they killed me. That's what seems true in my heart. So that must be what they did. Because they could not forgive me. They wrapped that bluebird in a cast of paraffin and set it aflame on an October night. Its ashy wings couldn't fly again.*

"Why do people do such horrible things?"

This question was asked by James Nairn, whose father had died in an explosion in the now-defunct mines of Copper Harbor. James had joined me the past few evenings by the outskirts of the piled black rocks. So had Alice and Evelyn Chambers, Thomas Thorne, and William McDonald. We couldn't invite the Swedish or Polish children because they didn't yet know English. James had never asked a question at our gatherings, not until now. His eyes were focused on a horror none of the rest of us could see, something that danced in the dwindling lights of the forest and pulled his pupils by a pair of invisible threads. It was impossible to tell whether he was listening for the answer, or whether he had asked the question only because he needed to ask it aloud, careless of what anyone would say.

The Reverend responded, but despite my distinct memory of so many of his other words, I cannot recall how he answered James. What I remember is the next story he told, on the final evening before the first stage of his transformation. It was the last time we children gathered to listen to his indecipherable sermons.

A great boat was built, to save all the creatures of the earth from a flood of fire. The boat was made of metal. This happened long before the time of Noah, back in a time when gods were capable of much greater anger. They have grown apathetic about us over the millennia, you see. That is why we cannot get the apocalypse we hope for. Our endings will not be worthy of any scripture, I'm afraid.

This metal boat was filled with cages, cunningly devised to keep the creatures from escaping, and to keep them from talking to each other too much. Eels were taught that eagles were demons. Cats became the archfiends of lizards. It came to be that none could understand each other anymore. Yes, truly, the designer of the metal ark was a genius, far more intelligent than Noah, his god more inspired than Yahweh.

The creatures all fought back against the confines and torture devices of the ark. All creatures except one, who finally adapted the ark to their own ends, who made a life of it. Do you know who this creature was?

We all shook our heads, sad, worried we were disappointing the Reverend with our ignorance, after he had devoted so much time to our learning in the days before his departure. Reflecting the dying embers of the fire, his eyes moistened. *Humanity. People.* He crossed and uncrossed his knobby knees. *They were the ones who embraced the ark. They are the children of metal.*

"Was the builder not a man?" I asked.

I don't know. I don't know if it was a woman or a man or some creature we no longer find on this earth. I only know that humans became the inheritors of the magical, mechanical boat that was constructed to save the world. He was dabbing his eyes with a sooty washrag. *To save the world by caging it.*

"Was the bluebird on this ark too?" Alice asked.

He was. Along with his would-be wife, his partner, his love. They became separated. For he thought he could outsmart the humans. He took their ways. He accepted a job. He kept the other prisoners in order aboard the ark. For all of these reasons, his wife could not forgive him, so she left. As soon as the ark was opened on the charcoal shores, she flew away, never to be seen again.

It was not until long after this separation, this eternal hurt, that the bluebird took to the gutters to save the young ones, that he repented of the part he had played in the op-

*eration of the ark. He always regretted what he had done
to make his playmate fly away.*

"Is it going to hurt when you transform?" I asked.

I expect it to hurt very much. In fact, I expect to die.

I couldn't stop the sobs from coming. None of us could.
We didn't want him to leave us.

Though our parents tried to keep us away, we all made
it to the shores of Deer Lake on October fifteenth, along
with those few, curious spectators who had nothing better to do: a woman with beady, reptilian eyes restrained a
bedraggled child by the strap of his overalls; a sunburnt
man sat on a boulder, cleaning dirt out of yellow, hooked
fingernails. The wind was howling and whipping the fly-
ers away.

The Reverend stepped into the frigid water, one hobble
at a time, stripping his clothes as he walked. At this out-
rage, the beady-eyed woman let out a gasp and yanked
her child away. The man with the grimy fingernails
grinned and rocked, his arms around his knees, perched
on top of his boulder.

He walked stark naked until the water had reached his
chin. Then he stood still.

He had told us this would be the difficult part: the pre-
freeze days. We mustn't speak with him. We must not visit the lake. The sparrows would bring him food, floating
it out to him on dry nests. He would need nourishment
until the time of his freezing. Then, once the weather was
right, they would pour water over his head each day, until the ice covered him from toe to head. He forbade us

from checking on him until the ice had thawed. He said he would need that time alone, undistracted by the needs of others.

On the day of the thaw, we all marched down to the lake. All of us except James, that is, who had begun working in one of the surface operations of the mine at Lake Medora. And Alice, who had died of cholera. She had fought as long as she could, sweaty and withering, eager to live long enough to see the Reverend's transformation. In the end the disease was stronger than her fervor. We placed a broken robin's egg on her grave.

Our parents told us we would find nothing in the lake. Nothing but rotting flesh nibbled by pike and trout. Nothing but the sad scraps of a foolish old man.

And they were right to an extent, of course. The Reverend's vacant eye sockets stared up at us from beneath the rippling surface. His slumped figure swayed, a weightless dancer entranced by the rhythm of the water.

We cried, long and hard, the tears burning down our cheeks. Nonetheless, sitting together in the rowboat, holding hands as he'd told us to do, we were unafraid. We were sure we would find out what had happened to him.

That evening, the talk of the town was how Anders Arvidson had shot a pair of blue herons that had arrived unseasonably early at Bete Grise Bay. On the porch of the general store he stood beside our parents, the feathered corpses slung over his shoulder, long necks jostling against one another. The company store had refused to purchase the herons at a fair price. Arvidson wanted to know who else would buy them, which was no one. He shouted about his wretched luck. Who would at least buy him a drink then? Who would buy him a meal?

We stood at the edge of the road, trembling, huddled against one another. The outline of the town, silhouetted by the red horizon, had transformed into the frame of a gigantic ship, sailing heedless over a scorched sea.

Why Don't We Add a Cozy Little Cabin?

~ Mike Robinson

Finally, after two years and just over a hundred thousand YouTube subscribers, Oliver Young felt comfortable enough to tell people what he really did. Although, when pitched the question in public, he rarely beat Angela to the swing.

"He's today's Bob Ross," she would say, usually leaning with one arm on his shoulder. "He's a one-man art school. Everyone digs his paintings."

Well, that was of course a lie, as heartening for her support as it was grating for its untruth. Like Bob Ross, he did landscapes on his channel—as indicated by the name, *Youngscapes*—though he aimed to add more dynamic variety, even a touch of the surreal. One of his more popular was the Atlantean ruins canvas, with a smoldering Pompeii-style volcano looming in the background. "Deviant" pieces, he sometimes called them. For the most part, his repertoire was forests and streams—quick mental escapes into Mother Nature.

Of course, a wider dragnet catches the delectable and detestable, and the trolls rode in parasitically on the backs of his fans. *Rip-off*, said some of the milder ones. *When you gonna paint some tits or something cmon it aint PBS.* Or those from the art world, so claimed, who with haughty diplomacy weighed in that he was another paint-by-numbers kind of guy—in short, a hack.

But it was no troll or critic that pushed him to the brink, that stripped over twenty pounds from him and reunited him with cigarettes and forced a wedge between him and Angela and remains responsible for his last upload being over six months ago.

It had actually been a fan. A fan who, as Oliver still claims, no less than saved his life.

For now.

As far as Oliver could tell, there was no other reason for it to have started during that episode, his 37th. Or why "it" (and who knew what "it" referred to) chose that canvas.

He'd been tired the night before and that morning and, even with two espressos in him, hadn't prep-sketched anything particularly interesting. Thus, the episode, already a day late for the weekly upload schedule set by his producer (also Angela), was going to be generic filler. Or, as they called it among themselves, a hand-warmer.

"Every once in a while it's good to recalibrate a little," he told the camera at the beginning of the episode. "To brush up on basics, and to appreciate the so-called 'normal' beauty of Nature." Palette in one hand, with the other he emphatically dabbed his brush toward the viewer. "And remember, as always, at the end I'll take a few calls for Q and A."

By then, the ending Q&A segments had grown from occasional to regular, a must for when he did live shows, which he'd been doing more of as viewership grew.

The scene he had in mind was simple: a forested river-bank with lordly Grand Teton-like mountains sawtoothed across the horizon. Snowcapped, of course. Maybe with bulbous clouds sliding over the summits. Like Ross, there was unabashed romance in his subjects, and in the way he approached them. Some used words like sappy or sentimental. 'Borderline schmaltzy' was one that had made him grin. He never thought twice about it, especially as he got older. If art gave you a sense of wonder or nostalgia, or even just that warm-cider-in-your-belly feeling, it was slowly, infinitesimally, diluting the poisons of the world.

For the first twenty-one minutes of his thirty-three-minute episode, nothing unusual happened. He had knifed in most of the evergreens, dabbed in the river and the riverbank and was about two-thirds of the way through the majestic visual sentence of the background mountains.

"You know what," he said. "I like this area. I might want a place to live here. So . . ." He moved down toward a clearing near the riverbank. "Why don't we add a cozy little cabin?"

To anyone watching (except that one fan, of course) the late idea to paint in a cabin appeared just as he intended it: a fun afterthought, a rustic punctuation mark of human habitation that temporarily fulfilled just another of Oliver's regular Thoreau fantasies.

Truth was, he'd no idea why the idea had felt so urgent, why the impulse to add his cozy little cabin had dizzied through him so primally, as if he'd been walking and, glancing down for the first time, realized he was mere feet from a cliff's edge and had to pull back.

Standing behind the lights and the camera, Angela looked concerned. He felt paler.

And though not really indicated by the close-up shot, his hand quivered that much more when laying down the roof and the wood panels and the highlights of the cabin. More detailed work always brought to his fingers the apprehensive tremble of his perfectionism—something which, privately, he hoped his live shows would subdue—but this was a colder, graver tremble.

He painted no doors or windows.

"Okay, there we go," he said, flashing a smile at the camera, then adding his own episode-ending catchphrase: "The world is now that much bigger."

Yes, one painting bigger. One vision bigger. One unit of beauty bigger.

The Q&A segment began. Callers ringing in from all over, so often lifting his spirit with every accent or strange new name, with the knowledge that he was making his mark, defying all borders and merging something of his spirit and imagination with so many others'.

He fielded three calls before taking hers. One concerned paintbrush sizes, another easel brands, another from London asked why it was that he couldn't get the snow right on his own "infernal mountains"?

Then came her call. A Joanne Bell. From Twilight Falls, California.

"Hi Ollie," she said. He noticed Angela's eyes widen at this unexpected show of familiarity. Only certain family members called him Ollie. "I don't have much time, really. But I wanted to make sure I got to you quick and clear—"

"Okay." His brow furrowed.

"I'm very glad you put a cabin in the painting," said this Joanne Bell from California. "And I'll bet you're glad, too."

Coldness rimmed his organs. He swallowed, his eyes narrowed a little and he maintained his smile. In later reviewing the footage, Oliver thought he actually looked pretty composed.

"I always like putting in those details," he said. There was no way he could keep the confusion from his voice, which seemed perfectly reasonable—who wouldn't be confused by the oddball statement?

"The problem is," Joanne continued, "you need to put a cabin in each of your pieces from now on."

"Pardon?"

"I'm a big fan and I don't want to scare you . . ." Joanne's voice seemed to volley between wise, middle-aged throatiness and a flightier youthfulness. There was a faint echo on her end. "But the cabin needs to be there. That's the only thing it'll recognize."

"Joanne, I'm n—"

"Oliver," she said, more forcefully. "It tried to come through you. But you contained it. And it *will* be contained. As long as the cabin is there."

"And what is it, exactly?"

No response, only dull electric click. Oliver shook violently now, a condition only worsened by efforts to suppress it. Some alarming, ambiguous truth rampaged within. His outer demeanor remained puzzled yet polite, no more than a twitchy dance of eyebrows and half-grins.

"Thank you, Joanne of California, for the ring," said Oliver. "I'm so glad you enjoy the show. Let's go to one more caller here . . . "

The last question came from Texas, an older man annoyed that "my palm trees never come out as good as yers." With a chuckle, the caller added, "They always look like dead spiders."

There was no saying when he awoke that night, because he never really fell asleep. Sleep had deserted him, leaving Oliver only with its mocking shadow, that loose dream-state that was more a brief dimming awareness, lit with the flashes of delirious little movies assembled by his tired, thought-wrung mind.

By two AM, Oliver found himself reanimating a motion he'd successfully stifled for almost a decade, but which right then felt eminently natural. He rose, dressed and left his house for the 7-11, on a tunnel-visioned task to buy a pack of Native Spirits.

He smoked one on the way back.

Only when he saw the porch light of his house again did something of his more conscious self, the Oliver of

Today, break through the relapsed automaton and realize that he'd forgotten his phone, that even in her sleep Angela had probably sensed the half-empty bed and woken up and flipped out (a little) and would even smell the smoke on him. Not that she was one to talk, having quit her "only do it with the girls" phase less than two years ago.

But the house remained dark and still. From the living room, he heard Angela grunt in her sleep. The darkness was like overgrowth, swallowing an old, abandoned building.

Second unlit cigarette between his lips, Oliver grabbed his sketchbook and pencils and stepped out onto the back patio, where he hunkered down on the couch swing and stared at the night and, with the click of the lighter, blew smoke at it.

His pencil hovered over the blank page. A muscle twitched in his forearm. Here he was alone, at home, surrounded by night shadow yet Oliver felt transported back to those childhood moments of drawing in public, when the act itself exerted its own gravity, pulling in those passing curious eyes eager to glimpse some unfinished creation.

Something now huddled over him.

With his third cigarette, the automaton took over again, and Oliver began sketching. He hadn't done faces in a while, and for good reason—they were never his strong suit. Nevermind portraits of actual people. But a good challenging hand-warmer always kept the dust from accumulating.

He drew Angela, best as he could. Or started to, anyway. Like the cigarette run, the choice had not been totally conscious, but the tug of a familiar current to which he found himself surrendering. Almost too easily.

He'd sketched in the basic framework—the spheres, the rough measuring lines—and had begun the features when some dull click in his brain made him pause, brought him to attention that whatever was coming through him or the pencil was not Angela but a thing with larger eyes and a larger mouth that, like an even more odious version of the impish kid who would pry into his drawing sessions to judge or direct, suggested itself in his every movement.

His trembling increased. His arm had become a wind tunnel amidst a hastening gale.

The cabin.

He wrenched his hand to the lower righthand corner of the page, where he quickly sketched the cabin: same height, some angle, no doors or windows. He couldn't tell if it was exact, of course, and his heart raced thinking that maybe he needed the same materials, the oils, the palette knife, the exact same strokes of the exact same measurements . . .

But, with the cabin crudely finished, all shaded and erect, Oliver's tremble weakened.

The cork in place.

Ash from the burning cigarette in his lips crumbled onto the page and slid off onto his lap. He shut the sketchbook, removed the cigarette and breathed.

☉

Angela stared at him from across the kitchen island, over the steam of her morning coffee. Perched on his stool, Oliver's gaze was mostly sunk in his bowl of soggy cornflakes.

"You believe that weird caller?" she asked.

"It's not about believing. It's . . . feeling. You saw me." He shoved a dripping spoonful into his mouth. "You told me I looked pale toward the end and I told you why."

"Ollie." Angela snorted. "Part of you never crawled out from under the bed. Mostly I find that endearing and I even love that about you. But—"

"Something took hold of me. Even before she called. I've never had a panic attack, I don't think, but I imagine it was on that scale. It was like a voiceless voice and it said, *Stop it it's coming stop it's coming stop—*"

"I know. I get it." Angela set down her coffee and crossed her arms. "All right, now I'm about to sound a little out there, but—what if she put those thoughts in your head? Before calling?"

Oliver studied her. "You mean, like telepathy?"

"Maybe. Or something more, I don't know, technical. Aren't there ways to focus sounds at people now? Like those Americans in Cuba that got sick that weird sound no one else heard."

Oliver shrugged, munched his cereal though he had no appetite. "Nothing about this feels technical. I feel cursed. In some . . . medieval way. And I don't know why. Or what."

Angela leaned forward on the counter. He saw in her eyes a certain caution he realized he'd not seen since their first date.

"And what's the deal from here on out?" she said. Her tone bothered him. It was cool, a little exasperated. The tone of a metal-boned businesswoman annoyed that the assembly worker's severed arm might *dare* delay the product. "Do you just paint woodland scenes with cabins? They didn't have cabins in Atlantis. And you can't exactly put cabins in your coral reef pieces. Or . . ." She leaned up, crossed her arms again. With a crack of humanity in her voice again, she said, "You stop the show, and stop painting?"

He bussed his half-finished bowl to the kitchen sink.

"No," he said. "I don't want that."

That afternoon, Oliver shut himself in his studio. He mounted a blank canvas and stared at it. Just days ago, the blankness would thrill and terrify him, in that exalted, sublime way he imagined skiers felt when gazing down an unblemished alpine run. Now the terror had crashed to earth, become a primordial thing that oozed and crawled.

And yet, the urge to paint, to draw, to reproduce himself artistically, had not diminished. It almost seemed to have grown, gaining heat in its own springtime fever. A heightened lust to engage and to spread.

In the righthand corner, he painted a cabin. Same size, same angle. He inhaled.

Exhaled.

In regarding the rest of the canvas, Oliver felt lightened. The unholy terror had lifted away once more to the realm of that sublime thrill-terror. The blankness was his again. And so, brush in hand, he began skating and skipping and swirling across it, becoming both watcher and doer.

He made a costal landscape, pine trees arrayed along a rocky beach, weathered cliffs sloping away into curling, crashing waves. The cabin was clearly not an organic part of it. But—had it freed him? Could he pass it off, in time, as just a quirky signature?

Oliver resented that he was even standing here doing and thinking all this. Why?

What had he done?

Biting his lower lip, he stared at the cabin. Something . . . bulged there, but not physically. There was a stirring that he could almost feel on a distinct, vibrational level.

With a mix of anger, curiosity and a burst of perhaps undue confidence, Oliver grabbed his palette knife, scraped up a sliver of yellow and leaned into the outer wall of the cabin—where, after a brief pause, he added a small, glowing window.

He recoiled a little. Watched. What breath he was holding he released in small, hiccuping sputters. Testing. Yes. Cautious. Reserving some in case—

—what?

Oliver wasn't sure how long he looked at his yellow dab of a window. The edge of his vision clouded over, some timeless fog encroaching on his senses, his seconds.

Eventually, he turned to wipe off the knife and wash the brushes. He almost didn't want to look again. But he did.

A tiny silhouette stared from the window. He could see nothing but the circular head and shoulders. He felt its gaze.

Shaking, he grabbed the palette knife, cut a line of brown and scraped out the window.

Then he hurried out the studio.

That she came from a small city—or large town, as it were—Oliver considered a hopeful sign. She was easy to find. There was only one Joanne Bell in Twilight Falls, California.

It had been a week since he'd set foot in his studio, the days a sludgy tide of Netflix and YouTube binging, solo hikes and smoking (about which Angela said nothing, as if long resigned to the habit's return), all blurred at the edges by a buildup of harried thoughts, willed distractions to outrun deeper thoughts, and the growing itch to paint.

Across social media, Angela made the announcement that *Youngscapes* would be going on hiatus. It was Oliver's idea to make a video of himself saying the same thing, to assuage any concerns he might be sick.

Though he did feel ill.

Less than ten minutes into Google and he had Bell's phone number, the one listed, anyway. He spent several more whiskey-smeared minutes following her name into

Facebook, where, again, the Twilight Falls signifier made for an easy trail.

As expected, she was an older woman, maybe early sixties, with gray curls and a melancholic smile. Oliver recognized her banner image as a version of a tropical waterfall grotto he'd presented on Youngscsapes maybe eight months ago. By the looks of it, she was pretty good. A little heavy-handed, but lightness came with practice.

She hadn't updated in over a month, and the top posts all appeared to be from other people.

. . . praying for you . . .

. . . in my thoughts every night . . .

. . . so wrong and so weird . . .

. . . ♥♥♥ . . .

He made his way down and found a post from a Diana Bell, blonde and visibly younger: *Thank you for all the support re: Mom. She's still in stable condition. I visit every other day and read to her as the docs think that helps (have heard that too). I think it does but may just be convincing myself. Doug and the kids come w/ me as much as they can. Trevor plays his flute for her.*

Scrolling further, Oliver came across a link to a Go-FundMe campaign for "Joanne Bell's Medical Expenses." A foreboding gathered around his mind which he tried to ignore. Diana Bell, presumably her daughter, had also posted a batch of Joanne's paintings—all landscapes, some direct copies or deviations of *Youngscapes* canvases, others more original. Multiple people had "liked" and "loved" and commented on the pictures.

. . . She loved her art. Was getting so good, too! . . .

. . . I remember during a picnic how she had to stop eating and sketch . . .

. . . Hopefully she'll be able to paint again . . .

One comment asked: *She has more recent stuff, right?*

To which Diana had replied: *She does. But I've decided not to post them. She became weirdly obsessed with doing cottages. Kept polluting her pictures with them and I wouldn't be able to say why. That was the first weird thing I noticed (though I didn't realize how crazy it had gotten) and I'm positive it had something to do with her current condition but we're all clueless. MRI and stuff were clean.*

Heart pounding, Oliver scrolled down and saw a post from Diana Bell from just over a month ago.

All friends and family: my mom Joanne is in the hospital. She is in a coma. Hard for me to even type those words. No one is sure what happened. It's a mystery because I know some of you were concerned since she kind of stopped posting here (she always loved posting her art) and truth be told I noticed odd behavior leading up to this but so far doctors aren't sure what caused her coma. They are thinking of transferring her to UCSF.

Only when it reached a certain threshold of bloodletting pain did Oliver realize he was biting his lower lip, and that a thousand muscles in his body were aching and taut. He kept scrolling.

He was both heartened and horrified to stumble across his own face, smiling back at him from what turned out to be the last thing Joanne herself had shared—the 24th episode of *Youngscapes.*

Smoking and pacing his backyard, Oliver waited four rings before she picked up.

"Mr. Young?"

"Call me Oliver," he said. "Or Ollie."

"Okay." Diana Bell sounded curt, guarded. Understandable. He was used to this demeanor now. Angela had affected it every day since they'd pre-empted the show.

"I appreciate you talking to me," he said.

"It's not big deal. You were one of Mom's favorite artists. Or channels, I guess. Thank you again for the kind words."

"Sure." The meat of the discussion, the very reason why they were on the phone together, grew thick and smoky and vortex-like between them. "So, I'm assuming you watched the episode I sent you?"

"I did." There was a shudder-breathed pause. "I don't know what to tell you. It certainly sounds exactly like my mom. Even though . . ."

Even though, Oliver's brain finished, she was in a coma by then.

"Something was wrong with her, leading up to it all," said Diana. "I feel cheated of closure, of any kind of explanation. What particularly disturbed me about what . . . 'she' said, I guess, to you was that she herself had started painting—"

"Cottages, right?"

"Uh huh. She was sort of a closet Thomas Kinkade fan. She liked nature, but also her quaint comforts. She even talked of retiring to some nice mountain cottage around here, near the redwoods somewhere. So she loved to paint her fantasy." Diana signed, a long sigh that contained the last few weeks. "And I thought she was getting obsessed with it. She would always have a cottage in her art, even if it didn't make sense. And she started adding more. Two, three. I didn't really understand at the time how crazy it got."

Flicking ash from his cigarette, Oliver watched the embers spark out and fade in the wet grass. "What do you mean, 'crazy'?"

Another pause. Oliver thought he could hear the hum of her hesitation.

"It'd be easier if I just showed you," Diana said. "Mind if I send you a few photos?"

His stomach tightened. "No, go ahead."

He put the phone on speaker and watched the screen, waiting, dragging long and slow on the cigarette, the smoke obscuring his vision and he thought how that might be good and that he ought to just hang up and even turn off the phone and put it away for now and then forever.

A text arrived. Then another.

And another.

He drew in a mouthful of smoke and held it as he opened the first text. It contained a picture of a canvas leaning against a wall—high cliffs, distant snowy peaks, pine trees.

And three identical cottages, in a row.

The second picture: a marshland piece, with six cottages arrayed across the bank.

Third picture: three open sketchbooks, littered with the same cottage, some in pencil, others ink, one in charcoal.

Fourth picture: no canvas, no sketchbook. Just a shot of a bedroom, its partially empty bookshelves, a dresser and a lone mattress and a glowing lamp throwing light on—

The walls. Where the cottage was everywhere. Manic wallpaper put up one repeating image at a time. The room felt like a braiding of determination and despair, the sweat-stride of prey running from pursuing jaws but deep down knowing the inevitable. It had the futility of someone trying to plug up every pore on their body, lest something get in.

But there were too many pores.

The weeks became months. Oliver increasingly felt like he was holding back a train. The desire to paint, to sketch, to doodle, to release something, anything, thickened in his veins, emotional plaque that even seemed to assimilate other more bodily desires—to the point that all of him became just a vessel for the passage of breath and the swelling press of this drive.

Though they had a decent amount of money in the bank, Angela insisted they both get "at least part-time jobs, if you want to piss away all we've built." By the third month, the fight had drained from Oliver, and he no longer responded to such comments.

He actually came to appreciate the distraction of looking for work. Though he took walks a couple times a day, which became multiple times a day, he had begun to feel useless and imprisoned. Funny, too, since, by the metric of sheer hours, he'd spent more time in his home when doing *Youngscapes*. But he had escapes then: magic brush rides into beautiful, fantastical Elsewheres that fulfilled him. Regular liaisons with his muse.

Surprisingly, he and Angela had more frequent sex. It was release, some kind, anyway, but the mood was different—disconnected and temperamental.

It was normally sometime in the post-coital hour, with the sweat cooling and aches subsiding, that Angela brought up nostalgia for *Youngscapes* and her desire to bring it back. "I still go through the socials," she said. "You got lots of fans waiting for you."

Oliver landed a part-time job at Hartmann's Market, two districts over. Mildly concerned about being recognized, even though it had only happened once, he considered asking that they not put him on cashier duty, yet he kept quiet.

A little over a week into the new job, Oliver burst from bed, consumed with the dream that had visited him. He'd been painting, as free and unencumbered as he'd been since that first time in his parents' garage when he was five. The endeavor had seemed wildly, dangerously unhinged, creations run amuck, world after vivid world.

"The cabin," he muttered half-consciously. He had to tame all the creation, otherwise it might slip through. Spill out.

He had managed to stumble down most of the hallway when the first bit of awareness struck him.

Where are you going?

By the time he'd woken up, he found himself poised over the kitchen island, elbows on the cold tile and pencil in his hand, quivering above a blank notepad. It took another few lugubrious seconds to convince himself he'd not actually drawn or painted anything. At that point, he'd done nothing in nearly half a year.

The clock read 3:36 AM. He didn't sleep that night, and called in sick to work the next day.

That afternoon, he received a call from Hartmann's manager, a pockmarked guy named Blake who Oliver wasn't sure was younger than he, and didn't want to find out.

"Hey Oliver," Blake said. "Sorry, I know you're under the weather, but I just found out about your YouTube channel. Holy cow! Amazin'!"

He frowned, tried to keep his voice lighthearted. "Who spilled the beans?"

"A customer. Regular. She recognized you, asked if it was you."

"It's me. I guess."

"Amazin'! Listen, I won't bother you further, but given this new info, how would you like to do some in-store murals for us? Same pay. But it would be your main focus. No stocking, no cash registers, nothing. For as long as it takes."

Oliver bit his lower lip. "Could I do what I wanted?"

"Well, within reason, sure. Why don't you and I chat about it tomorrow, during lunch?"

Closing his eyes, Oliver said, "Yeah. Um, sure."

"Amazin'!" said Blake. "See you then."

He dreaded sleep that night, but was pleasantly surprised to be granted five hours' worth. Few dreams came to him, at least those he remembered, though on waking around dawn Oliver had the vague impression of light flares in darkness, like muzzle-flashes across some deeper trench in his mind, and some thunderous thing strengthening.

Approaching.

"There's our resident arteest!" Blake said, arms outspread as he leaned back almost dangerously in his desk chair. Oliver stood in the doorway of the man's office. "Sit down. Let's rap."

Oliver sat on the edge of the office's only other chair.

"First things first," said Blake. Grinning with awareness of his own goofy positivity, he pushed a blank paper and pen over to Oliver. "I'm sorry to be like this, but you gotta give me a little sketch, and sign it. So I can retire well-off."

Taking the pen in hand, Oliver felt the swell of six months of pent-up expression, every urge that had come to him but had not left, forced into slumber but now stirring awake in his bones at this smallest and silliest of requests.

"Doodle whatever you want," Blake said. "So long as you sign it."

"Okay." Oliver touched pen to paper. "How about, um, a little cabin?"

Blake blinked. "Like in the woods? Sure. Whatever."

Oliver drew the cabin. Though rusty, his muscles had not forgotten their motion. Some small pressure lifted, but it was like a passage in fog, quick to be swallowed once more. His hand hovered over the paper.

Blake glanced over. "Did you sign it?"

His hand trembled. "I will."

"The world is that much bigger now," Blake said. "That's what you always say, right?"

Oliver hesitated.

"You okay, man? You look kinda pale. Still sick?"

With the best grin he could muster, Oliver said, "Let me add one more."

KNIGHT of WANDS.

Familiar Well

~ Eric Witchey

Slinky's best friend lived in the well behind the barn—the one with the rusty iron plate on top and the four locks at places around the edges like a compass. When someone hit her or took her toys or made mamma think she did a bad thing, she ran away from everyone and hid with her friend.

She had to be careful to run into the woods then circle back so nobody would know she came back and sat against the cold stones talking to Emmet. If anybody knew, especially Tilly who'd tattle a lie 'bout it, they'd likely try and kill him. They'd get theirselfs all excited and call him a water monster living in the poison well.

That's what everybody called Emmet's well—the poison well.

Even though all the sweet grass growin' tall around the poison well smelled more alive and tasted sweeter than anyplace else, nobody drank from the well. The farm had three other wells. Two were way far on the other side of the barn, the house, and the chicken field. Those were stone like Emmet's, but they didn't have tops and locks on them. The other well was pretty new and up next to the house and just a long pipe that went way down deep and deeper into the earth until it could suck up sweet water for the house and for keeping animals alive and all. That's the one they used the most. It was the one with a windmill that lifted water up into a tank on top of the house, and it was the one that put water in the troughs and sometimes even the pipes out into the corn-n-gourd fields when they got thirsty.

Emmet called that one a dead well because, "Nobody could live in a well that narrow. For good living, you need a deep stone well with a proper width and maybe a cave at the bottom."

She'd been sitting all quiet with Emmet a while after Tilly had done some mean thing to her when it occurred to her that maybe she didn't remember what Tilly had done. It wasn't tearing the head off her raggedy doll. That was last week. It wasn't hitting. She'd remember that because Tilly left bruises. It wasn't tattling a lie because if that had been it, she'd have heard her mamma calling after her, "Sylvia Jane Millicent Lancolm you get your ass in here, and you bring a switch with you!" Then, after some time of yelling for her, she'd hear, "Slinky! Come on in, Honey. It's okay, Baby. Come on back now."

Of course, she wouldn't. She'd never been that dumb since she was maybe three years old. Now she was eight, and she was practically all adult now. No way she'd be so big a fool as to go back until after dinner when Mamma would think havin' no dinner was enough for a stupid child who didn't know to take her lickings.

She chewed some sweet grass stems, tossed some pebbles at the barn, and named some cloud animals, but she just couldn't remember. "Emmet?" she said.

"Slinky?"

"Did I tell you why I come out here to sit with you?"

"No. You did not, Slinky. Would you like to?"

"I can't 'zactly remember."

"Maybe you just wanted to talk a bit with a friend."

She said, "Might be. You're a good friend."

"As are you, Slinky. If it weren't for you, I'd be terribly alone in this well. I was alone for a long, long time before we chatted the first time."

They sat in silence for a while. Slinky pulled a new stem of sweet grass and chewed the juice out of it. Finally, she said, "Are you a water monster, Emmet?"

"Don't know," he said. "Might be."

"How can you not know?"

"I'm not like you. That's for sure. I do live in the water, so that's a part of it. I'm probably not the one to say if I'm a monster."

"Well, somebody sure wanted you to stay in that well. They wanted it hard."

"Somebody sure did," he said. "They must have thought I was a monster, so maybe I am."

"I don't think you're a monster, Emmet."

"Me either, but I have to allow it might be true. They did go to some trouble to make sure I couldn't get out."

"Do you want to get out?"

Emmet was quiet long enough that Slinky wondered if he had something like sweet grass to chew on for thinkin'. Then, he said, "I think I'd like to look up and see the clouds again, and I think maybe I'd like to go in some different wells and maybe even a pond or a river. I think I used to like rivers a lot, but that was a long time ago. Now, this is my home. I don't think I would like to leave it for long."

"Some days, I think I'd like to leave home," Slinky said.

"Where would you go?"

Three pebbles at the barn later, she said, "I'd like to see Paris some days. I hear it's s'posed to be real nice."

"Is that a well maybe you'd like to visit? Or a river?"

Slinky chewed another piece of grass and flicked a pebble. "I guess it's probably more of a river than a well."

"That's nice," Emmet said.

Dinner that night was pretty good because Tilly weren't there and Mamma and Uncle Ralph and their baby, Reek, were all really quiet. Nobody yelled at her when she came back, so she figured they didn't remember any better'n her what Tilly done.

When she finished mopping up some gravy with her bit of bread, Mamma said, "Slinky, I need you to wash up tonight."

"Ain't it Wednesday? That's Tilly's night."

Mamma's face got pinched up like she wanted to yell a bit, but then it got smooth like it was too tired to stay scrunched up. Mamma said, "The doctor is coming for Tilly. I need you to pick up some chores so me and Uncle Ralph can talk to him."

"Tilly sick?" Slinky asked.

Reek made a wet sound like he always did, and Slinky thought maybe a water monster lived inside him, and then she almost laughed at the idea of Emmet inside Reek trying to talk through his belly button.

Mama said, "Real sick, Honey. Scary sick."

Real fast, Slinky said, "Okay, Mamma," because that was when she remembered why she'd run out of the house. When Slinky was scrubbin' the kitchen floor, Tilly called her "Chore Girl," so Slinky sassed her sister. That's when Tilly fixed to smack her with a fist again.

Slinky jumped up and backed off close to the back door. "I hate you!" Slinky yelled. As soon as she said it, a hot feeling came right into her feet and climbed up her legs. Scared worse, she screamed, "You're sick!" The hot snaked up over her hips, marched up her belly into her right arm then spit itself out the finger she pointed at Tilly.

Just like a shot squirrel, Tilly dropped on the clean floor and commenced to puking her guts out.

Slinky saw that, and she ran out the back door fast as she could. No way she was gonna stay around and get blamed for Tilly getting sick. It weren't her fault, and she weren't gonna clean that floor again nohow. She spent the whole afternoon hiding out with Emmet.

The next day and the next, the doctor came back. On the third day, the doctor told Mama he weren't coming back. No reason to. Nothing to be done. "The girl is past helping," he said. "Best to pray now."

That's what Mama, Reek, and Uncle Ralph all did, too. They commenced to praying like the devil had come to tempt them to sell their souls. Slinky seen them in the big room kneeling at the fireplace like it was an altar. Mamma reached out a hand for Slinky and said, "Come and pray for Tilly with us."

"Come on, girl," Uncle Ralph said.

Reek made a smell that made Slinky pretty sure a water monster really did live inside him, and that smell and all them scared eyes lookin' at her was enough for Slinky. She cut out for the woods, circled back, and settled to sit with her back against the cold stones of Emmet's well.

Without even plucking a stem of grass, she said, "I think Tilly is dying."

"Your sister?"

"Ain't no other Tilly here abouts."

"I suppose not," Emmet said. "What's killing her?"

"I don't know. We was fightin', and she took sick."

"Did you call for the doctor?"

"'Course we done."

Emmet kept quiet until Slinky said, "The doctor won't come by no more, and Mamma and Uncle Ralph and even Reek are all in the living room knee-beggin' to God."

Emmet stayed quiet. He was good at that. It probably come from bein' alone so much in the bottom of a well.

Cloud animals danced across the summer sky.

A couple of mourning doves darted from the barn and across the open yard to the woods.

Finally, Emmet spoke. "Before your Mamma's Mamma was born, and back when I could still go around to other wells and ponds and rivers, your Great Grandma, Selene, grew up here."

Her Greatgram's name made Slinky go all stiff. She looked around for some calamity comin' their way, and when she dint see nothin', she whispered, "Hush. We ain't s'posed to talk about her never, not ever."

Emmet said. "She was like you."

"You take that back!"

"Why?"

"I ain't like her."

"You take the time to talk to me just like her."

Slinky calmed down a mite. Nothin' bad had happened, and Emmet lived in a well, so he likely didn't know a lot of stuff. "Emmet, I don't know how to tell you this, but she was a witch. They come for her in the night, grabbed her, and burned her up."

"Somebody killed her?"

"I said she was a witch. She was hexin' people."

"What's a witch?"

It was Slinky's turn to be quiet. How do you explain a woman what fornicates with Satan to a thing that lives in your well? Finally, she said, "A witch is a woman with powers—a bad woman who hurts people."

Emmet said, "Oh. Then she wasn't a witch. She was always helping people. Once, she pulled water up from my well and boiled it to help a woman having her baby backwards."

"Really?" Slinky sudden-like felt bad asking because Emmet never lied to her, but everybody knew Selene was a witch and got burned for it. "She never hurt nobody?"

"Not that I know of. Once, she told me she pulled up some healing from the earth to fix a foal's leg. Another time, she said she had to touch a man who went stupid after his mule kicked him. She said he got mostly better."

"Mostly?"

Emmet said, "She said that men can be pretty stupid whether they're mule-kicked or not."

Slinky smiled, but it didn't change the fact that Great-grams had been doin' some hexy stuff. She said, "Them there's all powers, Emmet."

"Sure, she had some power," Emmet said. "But she wasn't a witch. She didn't hurt anyone. She only helped them."

Emmet didn't lie about things, and he didn't say stuff that didn't mean something. Slinky thought for a while about Greatgram Selene and how maybe some stories weren't so true as she been told. After some grass chewin' and some pebble plinkin', she said, "I wish she was here now. Maybe she could help Tilly."

Emmet answered quick—so quick Slinky thought maybe he'd been waiting for her to say just that. "Maybe there's somebody a lot like her who can help."

Slinky squinted at a cloud that looked a lot like a horse with wings. After deciding it needed more legs to be a horse, so it was more like a hawk, she said, "Who?"

"When you were fighting," Emmet said, "did you get really hot in your feet then the rest of you?"

Slinky didn't like to say so, but she said, "Yes."

"Then you," Emmet said. "You have the feeling in your blood like your Great Grandmother."

"No."

"Yes. That's why we can talk. That's why you can go in the woods and nobody can follow your trail. That's why even if they look right at you from the barn, nobody can find you sitting right here next to me."

"Hidin' ain't hexin'."

Emmet ignored her and said, "And that's why Tilly got sick."

Slinky jumped up and ran away. She wanted no more of Emmet telling her she might be a witch and get burned.

After dinner, she saw her sister wide-eyed scared and near to dying in her cot. That's when she started to thinkin' maybe she might listen to Emmet a bit more. Slinky cleared the table and did the dishes real slow so Mamma, Reek, and Uncle Ralph got settled by the fireplace for Uncle Ralph's smokin' and thinkin' time.

Slinky slipped out to talk to Emmet.

Under the paintbrushy splatter of stars across the sky, she rapped on Emmet's iron plate. "You awake?"

"I'm here. Are you okay?"

She tried not to let him know she was half cryin'. "Tilly's real bad sick."

"Yes," Emmet said.

"Can you tell me what to do? What I did? I gotta make it right."

Emmet said, "Close your eyes."

She did.

"Feel down through your toes right through the grass and into the ground. Like a big old oak tree, root your heart down into the warm rivers of life flowing in the earth."

She remembered how it felt when she got mad and pointed—all that heat running up her body like a river. Wiggling her toes, she reached with her feeling heart down and down and . . . and there it was, down in the ground, down where the blood of the world flows and moves the livingness all 'round the earth.

She wiggled her toes again, and the warm come right up into them like she was standing in a yesterday's storm puddle under hot August sun.

"Now," Emmet said, "take hold of the South and East padlocks on my lid, one in each hand."

She didn't dare open her eyes cause the river of livin' might disappear, so she fumbled until she gripped the two locks.

"'Good, Slinky. Now, let the flow move into those locks so they know what you want."

The river of heat come up her legs and belly. It moved like water through her arms into her hands and into the iron locks.

Those locks remembered that before the forge they was sand in the ground, and they snapped themselves free and fell away like Uncle Ralph had hit them with a sledge.

Her eyes snapped open, and she looked at her empty hands. On the ground at her feet, the locks melted away into red sand that just sank down into the earth and was gone. "I broke 'em," she said. "Oh, God. I broke 'em just like I broke Tilly."

"No, Slinky," Emmet said. "You helped them go home. You helped me, and you're going to help Tilly." Where the locks had been, the near edge of the iron plate bulged upward, bent a bit, and lifted. Two brilliant yellow cat-slit eyes caught starlight.

Slinky jumped back.

"It's okay," Emmet said. "It's just me." A flat, glistening red-black head pushed outward. A four-toed hand pulled on the edge of the well. With a pull and wiggle, a long, flattened, glistening body and tail followed until the whole slick Emmet plopped down on the grass between the well and Slinky.

A little afraid and a little curious, Slinky touched a finger to Emmet's head. Her finger found cool, damp skin. She said, "You ain't no monster. You're just a real big salamander."

Emmet chuckled. "I've been in the well a long time."

"Should you be out? Folks might gonna notice a slick salamander big as a panther slitherin' round."

"Yes," He said. "But I'm your salamander just like I was Selene's."

"I'm not sure that's so good an—"

Emmet lifted a four-toed front foot to hush her. "A nice thing about being your salamander is you can make me look like whatever you want."

She remembered the scared and maybe gonna die look on Tilly's face in the cot, and she decided that helpin' was maybe better'n arguin' just now. "Well, we gotta do somethin' if you're gonna help Tilly."

"You, Slinky. I'm going to help you."

She put her hands on her hips like Mama and wished she had her a wooden spoon, too. "You mean help me help Tilly. Right?"

"Of course." Emmet lifted his broad, flat head and fixed his yellow starlight eyes on her. "What do you think I should look like?"

"Maybe a boy my age or a dog or somethin' that fits in 'round here."

Before she could think of something else folks wouldn't notice too much, Emmet stood up on his hind legs and commenced to melting all over and to twisting like he was made of chink mud and to shifting some and lifting some and stretching some until he was a barefoot boy a bit taller than Slinky and wearin' an old-time Sunday suit with a tall hat, a string tie, a split-tail coat, and a silver watch chain. Even though the suit crumpled up on him like it was hands-me-down from an older brother or cousin, it seemed like a fittin' in thing for him to be wearin'.

His smile went all wide and starlight bright and full of joy and life. His big yellow eyes sparkled like shooting stars. "Thank you, Miss Slinky. Thank you ever so very much." He took her hand in his four-fingered boy hand and kissed it like she was a lady in a story.

Slinky jerked her hand back. "You Satan?" Sayin' it, she knew she kinda hoped so 'cause she figured she knew enough stories to figure out how to sell her soul to fix what she done to Tilly. She hoped she didn't have to fornicate with Emmet's salamander self.

"I am certainly not," Emmet said.

Slinky relaxed a bit. "Then what zactly are you?"

"I am part of that living earth feeling you can touch, and you decided to see me like this."

"I did not. I would not turn some old salamander into—"

Emmet's deep laugh interrupted her.

She stared at his all-happy face in the starlight.

When he caught his breath from laughing, he said, "We'll talk the how and what of things later. Right now, listen to me if you're going to make Tilly right."

Slinky went quiet.

Emmet said, "I'll lift up the well cover a bit, and you draw out some water."

"We can't slip a bucket under there. It's too tight."

"We don't need a bucket. Just a bean tin and a long bit of baling twine from the barn."

Slinky kenned him right away. She ran and gathered up the stuff then they dipped up some water.

Slinky, holding that bean tin full of well water like it was made of liquid gold, let the frumpy-suit Emmet boy lead her toward the house with him whispering in her ear all the way.

A few days passed after Slinky life-warmed that cup of water from the poison well and gave it to Tilly. Come a mid-afternoon, Slinky ran away 'round through the woods to the well. Of habit, she set down with her back against the circle of stones, knowing true that Emmet had gone on and away after they healed her sister.

Slinky was bustin' to tell him Tilly was all fixed now and a lot nicer, and she had to tell somebody she felt a little bad about that 'lot nicer' bit. She worried maybe the hexin' made Tilly a bit not who she used to be.

"She is." Emmet's voice near scared her dead even though it come right up from the well just like always. Slinky jumped away and twisted around until she was on her hands and knees starin' at the iron cap and the stones.

Emmet said, "Now, she just knows better than to hurt you."

"You came back!" Slinky crawled across the grass and hugged the stones of the well, and she was pretty sure she'd'a hugged Emmet himself even if he come up out the well as a slick-skinned, panther-sized salamander.

Emmet said, "Took a long walk is all. Visited the river and the pond. Looked in on the other wells."

"Just like you said."

"Of course. I told you this was my home."

"Yes. Yes, you did." Her face heated up a bit, but not full of the living heat, just with the embarrassment of forgetting that Emmet never lied to her.

"Slinky?"

"Yeah, Emmet?"

"Would you mind breaking off the other locks and taking the iron cap off a while so I can see the sky?"

"Sure enough, Emmet. Right now." She come close up and grabbed the North and West locks, one in each hand, and commenced to conjuring up some livin' and lock rememberin' from the earth.

"Don't break them so much as the other ones," Emmet said, "We'll want to put the lid back on and hang the locks like they aren't broken."

She kenned him quick and slowed down her conjurin' to make sure the locks didn't get too excited about bein' sand again.

Once she slid that lid off, she sat down against the stones. Emmet come up out the well enough to get his wide, flat head up on the stones by her shoulder. Quiet and happy, they watched the clouds together.

Eventually, Emmet said, "In a few years, I think we should go to Paris."

Slinky smiled. "I'll be growed all up then." She watched a cloud goose chasin' a tick hound across the sky then said, "You think you'll grow into that suit of yours?"

"If you want me to. You think I should wear it to Paris?"

"Yup. I think it's just the thing."

Emmet asked, "How far will we have to swim to get there?"

Slinky plucked a stem of sweet grass and chewed it for a while. Eventually, she come to think maybe she should explain about Paris being a city and not a river or a well. Instead, she said, "If we was clouds, we could fly."

Emmet said, "There's a lot of water in clouds."

Slinky smiled, wiggled her toes into the grass and dirt, pulled up some life into her toes, pointed up at that 'ol dog-chasin' goose, and pushed and pulled the conjurin' on that goose just enough to get her wings flappin'.

Satisfied, she let the goose go on across the sky after the dog. In a couple years, she'd about have flyin' figured. That was plenty of time to explain Paris to Emmet. Slinky sucked in the lazy smell of summer heading on toward harvest and pulled herself a stem of sweet grass to chew.

QUEEN *of* CUPS.

Halos

~ *D. Thea Baldrick*

*"Every morning the old woman . . . cried,
'Hansel, put out your finger, that I may feel
if you are getting fat.' But Hansel always
stretched out a bone, and the old dame,
whose eyes were dim, could not see it,
thinking always it was Hansel's finger."*
—Hansel and Gretel, 1887

Deep in the woods, bisected by Route 27, in a house found only by invitation, I have a lab with sixteen avian species and a firebird. One cage on the floor sits empty with the latch undone and the door open. Upstairs I have a room with mice. The aquariums are in the basement.

Gretel came often to sit among the birds and to read or watch. Hansel was too afraid, or too wise, and never returned, but his sister was there on the day I poured agar into petri dishes for the new bacteria. I made hundreds of petri dishes at a time. When they cooled, I put them in the refrigerator. After a few days, I would take them out for inoculation.

"Old woman, old woman, old woman, says I," Gretel said between bites of the apple I had left for her. She was sitting curled up in my armchair, an open book in her lap, "What does this mean? I don't understand."

"Nobody does," I said, "Probably." It was a non-answer, but I was busy.

"But you haven't looked."

"It doesn't matter. The level of understanding remains the same."

"Look," she insisted.

It was the equation that I was always scribbling down, in margins, on the end leaf, in the condensation on the window, or in the ashes in the fire. Once I amused myself by having an orb weaver incorporate it into his web. It took surprisingly little manipulation of the spider's brain. "That means," I told her, "that based on evolutionary theory, what we see is not real and what's more, cannot be real. Reality, as we see it, is an impossibility."

There was a long silence. I went back to work.

Finally, she said, "If that is true, what is reality?"

"That would be the right question."

"And what would be the right answer?"

"I don't know."

Exasperated, she shut the book with a clap. The birds fluttered in their cages, the firebird repositioned herself and Gretel came over to watch me pour.

"Stand back," I said. "It is easy to contaminate this."

She stepped back. "What are you growing this time?"

"*Staphylococcus stravinski.*"

"What is it for?"

"It grows on bird feathers. I am adding two genes that I have designed."

"To the bird feathers?"

"No, no, to the bacteria. It's too difficult to add them to the bird. I would have to wait too long for the results."

"So why are you adding the genes?"

"I am, for obvious reasons, interested in aging. The first gene should make the bacteria live longer. The second gene turns the bacteria gold, so I know which bacteria I have tampered with."

When she left, she had the temerity to hug me, and as she walked through the woods, I could hear her singing, "Old woman, old woman, old woman, says I, oh whither, oh whither, oh wither, so high?"

Silly girl.

The next time she came, she was older, and I was not. She gained on time with a remarkable speed, and yet, I know her own perception was that time passed with an excruciating slowness. I hardly aged at all from one point to another and yet time fled from me at a rate I found breathtaking. That observation has kept me up at night, thinking.

"Old woman," she said as she peered in at the birds, who all had gold feathers, except for the firebird, "Do you think they are happy in the cages?" She was eating another apple. As usual her questions were flavored with apple chunks and saliva. The birds were pecking at their seeds. The aquarium creatures were picking at bloodworms and plankton. The upstairs mice nibbled on pellets. Everything was eating all the time.

"The feathers are infected now with the *Staphylococcus stravinski,*" I said. "If the birds flew away, what do you think might happen?"

"I suppose the bacteria would end up in the wood and, if conditions were right, they would grow and multiply out in the world."

"Yes, that is a possibility," I said.

"So, it is important to keep them in cages until we know more?"

"The doors are unlatched."

"They are?"

"The birds could leave if they wanted to."

"Maybe they don't know they can. Maybe they don't know what's real?"

I shrugged, "Maybe. No more than we do."

"Maybe," she said, opening the door to the sparrow's cage, "maybe they just need to be shown."

I said nothing. I was, in truth, deep in my project. I may or may not know how to turn a blind eye, but I caught a glimmer of gold as the sunlight flashed on the bird as it flew through the door.

"Well, you did it," I said, glancing up from the microscope.

"Is it OK?" she asked, her hand on the raven's cage.

"Probably not," I said, turning back to the microscope.

The raven, too, flashed bright in the sunlight, its delighted caws growing faint as it flew through the wood and over Route 27.

Days, weeks, perhaps a month later, Gretel appeared in the doorway, bringing too much sunlight, disturbing my new collection of birds. She had let all the previous ones loose, all but for the firebird who stubbornly remained in her cage despite the open door. The new lot blinked at the infusion of light, but even as the girl shut the door behind her, the room remained too bright. I realized, as I looked up, that the gold glow was from her hair.

"Oh, dear," I said, laughing. "Oh, dear, my dear, oh, dear." I was almost in tears. It was just too funny. "You're infected."

"Yes," she said grimly.

"Serve you right," I said, smiling, turning back to the centrifuge which had just finished spinning. I opened the lid and took out the microtubule and peered at the pellet that had formed at the bottom.

I took another peep at the girl. "Oh, dear," I said, chuckling again. The glow was concentrated around her scalp where the bacteria would have formed in thicker quantities near the new growth of the hair follicles.

"Actually," I said, peering at her more closely, as I put on my strongest pair of glasses. "This is interesting. Cross-species contamination. Do other animals have it? Horses? Deer? Dogs? Cats? Mice?" She was shaking her head. "What about other primates?"

"I don't know," she said, "But that's not the issue."

"It must have mutated to infect humans," I mused, "But why? The evolutionary advantage must have been extreme compared to other animals." I stared at her, thinking.

"My dear old woman, I am trying to tell you—"

"Length of life!" I cried. "The birds didn't live long enough for the bacteria. With its enhanced lifetime, it needed a host who lived at least as long as it did. And you're a convenient host, there are so many of you. Mystery solved. Not so interesting anymore." I went back to the centrifuge.

"You are not listening to me."

"No," I muttered as I carefully decanted the microtubule.

"Look at me, please."

I looked.

"What do you see?"

"I see a skinny girl, far too serious, with a thin face, a broad nose and really rather lovely skin, with a heavy infestation of genetically modified *Staphylococcus stravinski* on her head."

"Well, other people see a halo."

"A halo!" Oh, dear, I had to sit down.

"Yes, and what's more, only some people get it. It's everywhere, all over the world, but some people are immune to it."

I nodded, still chuckling. "Of course."

"The problem is that it has become a sign of holiness. Cults are forming. The science people have pointed out that it is microbial, but they're drowned out by all the furor. Look at it. It is rather dramatic. And things are getting ugly. Elitism. Prejudice. There's been violence.

"Really?" I said, getting up to return to my project. "So what else is new?"

"Old woman! You have to do something!"

"Why?" The liquid I decanted needed to be put in the thermocycler.

"Because you can!"

"Maybe I could, that's true, but the stupidity of what is going on out there beyond the wood does not interest me. At the moment, getting this into the thermocycler interests me."

"But you started the whole thing!"

"Did I?" I said, glancing at her.

The girl cried out with frustration or guilt. As she grabbed her hair, sparks of gold flew out and I stepped back. I did not want to become infected myself. A halo would be even more ludicrous on me. My sisters would enjoy the irony far too much.

"If it matters to you so much, you fix it," I said.

"Me? How can—"

"What you need to know is here." I waved at the bookshelf. "What you need to do is here." I indicated the lab equipment.

"The firebird might help," I said as the bird changed its position in its sleep. I looked at it thoughtfully. "For some reason, the bacteria dies when I put it on her feathers. It is not without interest. If I weren't so embroiled with this new project, I would look into it myself."

I really had to put the liquid in the thermocycler. As I was walking away, I mentioned, "Oh, by the way, the effect probably won't last forever. I am not sure how the bacteria will work on the different keratin in hair, but it is likely that it has the same effect as on birds. It is a feather-degrading bacteria. Keratin is its food source. Once its food source is gone, the bacteria will die. Probably. Unless of course it adapts to include another source of keratin. Like skin. The extended lifespan has obviously given it enhanced adaptability mechanisms it didn't have before."

"You mean that once it's eaten my hair and I'm bald, then it will start on my skin?"

I shrugged. "Maybe."

After I ran the thermocycler, I turned to find her sitting cross-legged on the floor, flipping frenetically through books she had pulled from the shelves: Biochemistry, Pathophysiology, Bacterial Pathogenesis.

"You've written all over these," she said.

"You can, too. Just use a different color."

She may or may not figure out how to remove halos from the world, but what's more important, by the time she's done, I'm going to have a nice little lab assistant. If she can't figure it out and the yellow glow continues to annoy me, I may have to show her how to remove it myself. It's fairly simple. Everything eats something. It's just a matter of engineering something to eat the bacteria. A virus would do nicely.

The Ducks Opened the Hostilities

~ *Mattia Ravasi*

The ducks opened the hostilities by murdering my cat.

I'd seen them loitering around the edge of my back garden all week. The fence along the right side had sunk in the mud during Winter; there were several spots along the bottom where the pests could squeeze through. A handyman was supposed to come look at the fence in April, but then the dreadful business with the virus occurred, and no one showed up.

I was leaning over the breakfast counter, sipping my coffee and scrolling through emails on my laptop. I looked out between a message and the next, checking on Kipfel. His back was straight and low to the ground, and he was staring at the trees at the back of the garden. I thought he'd found a vole. He loved gutting the little things, but couldn't manage it without getting scratched and bitten, and moaning for me to take him to the vet.

I didn't register what was happening—I was reading an email from my manager, badgering me to start using the latest ghastly software the company had purchased to "speed up our march to modernization," and make our jobs easier to outsource—until I heard Kipfel hiss. Perhaps that was how he roared. Perhaps he was already in pain.

When I looked up, he had a duck in his claws. Four other birds had their beaks on his tail and hind legs. His tail was shaven—he'd had eczema recently—and must have been very sensitive. He gave up easily.

They hammered away, pecking wherever they could reach, not leaving him enough air to hiss again. I could hear this wet piercing noise all the way through the double glazing. The attack put me in mind of a scene from one of those very serious, very violent American dramas my colleagues were always raving about, one that I'd started watching during lockdown. This tall fat Mexican is crossing a prison cafeteria, when suddenly four skinheads surround him, and start puncturing him with shivs made from sharpened toothbrushes.

Shiv shiv shiv, made the toothbrushes in the Mexican's guts, going in and out like a sewing machine through a skirt.

Shiv shiv shiv made the beaks into Kipfel.

I stood, horrified, howling noiselessly, looking not quite at the massacre but just to the side of it. I said to myself that it was too late to intervene, although this was perhaps a lie, told in self-defense or out of cowardice.

They didn't eat him. When I could force myself to walk outside, I saw that his fur was matted with blood, but he was otherwise intact. He was an old cat. Perhaps his heart stopped from fear alone.

The ducks had disappeared into the trees. There's supposed to be a fence at the back of those, too, and that one isn't sunken or torn, to my knowledge, but I didn't have the guts to go and check.

☉

I called the handyman to see if we could schedule a new date for repairing the fence. He didn't pick up. I tried again over the next few days, to no avail.

I told Peter about it when I next emailed him. Discussing the event, however briefly, helped me process my grief and fear. I asked him if the ducks' behavior was normal: he's supposed to know a lot about poultry.

He replied somewhat prissily that what I had were probably mallards. *If I were there, Deborah, I would fix that fence*, he concluded. *I would protect you.*

I have had my share of gentlemen pining after me. I was once considered, if not a great beauty, at least "a fit bird," as a hirsute Geordie once described me to his mates in the Trout pub. In my experience, the most romantic men are also the most predatorial. They will jump on any chance to make their feelings known, however cowardly and obliquely, and will reiterate their existence at every turn. You can't tell them about your mauled cat without them proposing they move in with you.

I think what made me such a fit bird was a certain degree of exoticism. My family moved to England from a Bayern town called Deggendorf in 1963, when I was eight. Apparently, I took the move badly: I resented leaving the cozy microcosm of our tiny town, with toy stores, boutiques, and bakeries just downstairs from our apartment, in favor of the empty countryside outside Oxford. My parents used to relish their memories of my childish angst, but I remember nothing of Deggendorf at all.

How exotic could you be as a West German in England, you may ask. Quite a bit. There weren't many non-English families around, not in 1970 Yarnton. Oxford itself had a faint claim to cosmopolitanism—nothing like what it is today—but the foreigners there all belonged to the university, which made them as untouchable as their English blokes. They weren't Australian or Mexican: they belonged to the egalitarian nation of the posh.

My hair was a different blonde than the other girls'. I had wider cheekbones, and I was taller. The recent crimes of my nation fascinated people, who looked at me with great curiosity, pondering the ungaugable depths of human evil.

Melvin was the first boyfriend who didn't study my face that way. Some days he watched me in adoration. Other times he barely glanced my way, especially when Tottenham was playing. All my life I have been plagued by the most uncomfortable thoughts, and one that used to bring me great misery was a suspicion that perhaps my love of Melvin was founded on this basic fact: that he took me for granted, and never thought of me as special.

The fear has gone now, as all my fears, no matter how rancid, eventually do. Looking back on them is always a sorry business. I contemplate the anxiety and sadness they caused me, and weep for all that lost serenity. So what if that's why I loved him? As if we can even figure out the mechanics of such a maddening thing as love.

After we got married, Melvin and I bought a house in Binsey, where I still live. It's a small village perched just beyond the marshy fields of Port Meadow, a half-hour walk from Oxford city center. Not that I go into town much these days, what with the plague and all.

Two days after Kipfel died I put my mixing bowl on the scale and measured out 750 grams of strong baking flour. I mixed in yeast, salt, a tablespoon of sugar, and a bottle of rat poison. I poured in half a liter of water, lukewarm from the kettle, and kneaded the mixture till it got plump and stretchy, slamming and slapping and folding it on the floured table. Baking is hard work, if you do it properly. I covered the dough with a cloth and left it to raise for an hour in the cupboard by the boiler.

This course of action caused me great distress. I wasn't facing any moral dilemma (one way or another, the ducks must go), but the plan required me to sacrifice an awful lot of flour. These days, that stuff is worth its weight in gold. It disappeared altogether from supermarket shelves early during the national lockdown. The local mills, from which I shop, all had to close down, unable to cope with demand. (One of them, in Islip, published a confusing post on their archaic website, rambling about a "raid" they had been subjected to.) The luxury delis, which abound around Oxford, only stock extravagant varieties, like seitan or stone-milled quinoa, going for ten, twelve pounds a kilo.

Not that I had any first-hand experience of empty aisles and cut-throat delis. I only knew about it from my colleagues' chitchat, and from their increasingly worried updates during the Team Tea Breaks we were forced to attend remotely every Wednesday afternoon, to Foster Corporate Camaraderie and Keep In Touch.

I scoured the table with cleaning products while my poison loaf was in the oven. I left it in longer than needed, to make it extra crusty. I let it cool until the evening, then smashed it into crumbs.

I turned the garden lights on and scattered the crumbs in piles all around. I was terrified. I'd been studying the garden through an upstairs window, peeping from behind the curtain to make sure the coast was clear, but my mind still latched onto every stretch of darkness, those draped between the trees and the vast endlessness beyond the fence, transforming them into the contours of dripping, probing, pustulent monstrosities, lashing out to torment me.

The final pile of crumbs I left just under the trees at the back of the garden. It was the furthest I'd been from the house since the beginning of lockdown. All my groceries had been delivered by exhausted Sainsbury's drivers, the apples and bananas carefully picked for maximum bruises.

☉

I work in academic publishing. I assist the editors of scholarly journals, make sure we publish the occasional issue to schedule, and that we don't go too crazy with the page budget. I follow the directives of the manic-depressives in our editorial department, whose job, as I understand it, is to go on two-week work retreats to Scotland, and to strike publishing deals that we will never be able to honor over drinks and blow in SoHo clubs.

The academic editors I work with vary greatly in personality, from the exquisite to the oblivious to the violently abusive. Many of them work in academia because they lack the basic survival skills that would ensure their success in any normal field of employment. Had they been born in Barnsley, they would be pushing tinned tomatoes across the bottom shelves in Aldi—assuming Barnsley's Aldis, unlike the local ones, are still well-stocked and operating—but because they aced the parent lottery, they became the deans of All Souls instead.

Peter sits somewhere in the middle of the spectrum. He's imperious and curt, intolerant of mistakes although frequently blundering himself, prone to panicking if his emails aren't instantly acknowledged. Yet he is in love with me, which dulls his sharper edges, and gives him a certain drippy niceness.

I only met him once, at an editor meeting in 1989. He was annoyed about certain late issues, and I don't think he looked me in the eye throughout the meeting. At the time, our correspondence was all handled via post and fax: article proofs would be mailed, corrections returned in incomprehensible scribbles I would then transliterate and forward to our typesetter. Maximum chances for error at every step. Then, sometime in the mid-00s, email became our medium of choice, we transferred all our data into cranky, byzantine tracking software, until finally, in 2016, the company cut back on office space, and introduced its semi-forced homeworking policy. They were years ahead of the curve, it turned out.

Peter's feelings became clear around that time, first through veiled hints I could still choose to disregard, later via blatant declarations worded carefully enough not to hold up in court, in case I reported him for harassment. All these years I've never known what brought along the change in him. Perhaps my email personality is different from my handwritten one. My hands get cramped easily, and I never stretch a letter longer than I must, but I'm very wordy on a keyboard. Perhaps emailing editors from my kitchen and living room collapsed that professional distance that existed when I was still commuting into my depressing cubicle, where decorations were only allowed if they bore the company logo. I might have become friendlier in my greetings and farewells, and certain men—I don't assume Peter has had much experience with the ladies in his six decades on Earth—latch onto any kindness that is shown to them as an excuse to fall in love, and give the misery of their life the sexy sheen of unrequited passion. Perhaps Peter has loved me since 1989, and that's why he couldn't meet my eye during that meeting: the heat of my gorgeousness would scorch his eyes, and wet his pants, if he witnessed it directly. He had been waiting ever since, and only made his first move a respectful few years after my husband passed away in 2014.

I've been dying to ask him, but it would be too cruel. Showing any interest would only stoke his hope.

I don't love Peter back by the way, bless him. I don't wish him any harm, but he's a bit of a twat.

When I woke up the next morning I looked into the garden, and saw dead magpies close to two of the crumb mounds. No sign of the ducks.

I let out a very crass German expletive when I walked into the kitchen. I'd thought I could hear sounds in the night, but I'd imagined them to be rooted in my dreams, and there was no way anyway that I would leave my locked bedroom while it was dark.

I saw muddy prints all around the floor. The cupboard door under the counter had been pulled open. The food inside had been strewn all around, but most of it seemed uneaten: potatoes, carrots, a sad withered leek. Then I noticed that my biscuit tin had been opened. I bake shortbread every Sunday afternoon, to have with my crime novels on the couch before going to bed. There had been five days' worth of biscuits in that tin. The intruders vacuumed them all up, leaving no crumb behind.

The prints all converged on the cat flap in the kitchen door.

I sealed the flap shut using an entire roll of duct tape. Duck tape? Ha. Lately I've been wondering if I'm completely sane.

Then again, haven't I always?

I baked a loaf of bread for my dinner that afternoon. I spent the entire night on the loo. I was certain that my putrefied body would be found on the bathroom floor seven months from now, calcified waste still crusting the toilet bowl, testifying to the agony of my final moments.

I suppose some traces of rat poison must have lingered in the oven, and that I ate them with my bread. Smashing. If my oven was out, I wasn't sure how long I'd survive. I didn't have much food around the house, except for those bags of strong flour, and I doubted I'd be able to get a food delivery. All that my colleagues seemed to talk about these days was how hard it had gotten to book a delivery slot.

At the apex of my agony, when it felt like the cramps were tearing a hole through my gut, I dialed 999. I waited an eternity with my phone pressed to my ear. These days my joints are so sore even holding the phone to my face is painful, but the distress was a welcome distraction from the harsher burning in my bowels. Nobody answered. This is preposterous, I thought. How bad can this virus be, that they can't spare a nurse to answer 999 calls? I blamed the Conservative and proto-Conservative governments that had stripped the National Health Service of its resources. I blamed the 999 operator, which I imagined as a chavvy young woman posting pictures of herself on whatever ghastly app was popular this week, ignoring the LEDs flashing red on her terminal. I blamed the ducks.

The next morning I reported the whole accident to my colleagues in a long, somewhat rambling email. (I'm not usually one for reaching out to colleagues, be it for comfort, support, God forbid chitchat.) I left out the turbo-diarrhea, but stressed my indignation at the lack of response from the emergency services.

I must have shocked them, I thought around noon, when I saw that nobody had replied yet. But nobody ever replied to that email.

That the world was still there I could testify by climbing the ladder to the attic—no small feat, let me tell you—and looking through the tiny round window up there, which overlooks the neighbor's houses and the hedge-lined fields beyond, and gives me a view, very far in the distance, of the tiniest segment of the A34 speedway. I could see vehicles driving up and down. Trucks, mostly, with the occasional car.

Those thoughts I mentioned, which used to cause me such a great deal of pain, remained a terrifying mystery to me until the day I attended a 10 am editor meeting in a drab, dark pub just outside Paddington Station. I was meeting the chair of some psychology society, trying to persuade them to keep publishing their journal with my company.

It was clear from the start that I would make no progress, and that the bloke was only meeting me as a professional courtesy. I didn't resent him. I always considered my company cheap and unprofessional, and my opinion of him instantly improved when I realized he was abandoning us.

I had traveled all the way to London, and going back too early would mean having to spend the afternoon in the office. Even though we had no deal to strike, I asked the bloke if he wanted to join me for lunch. On me: a farewell gift from his old publisher.

We ate fish and chips—back then it still tasted proper, none of this modern gastropub beastliness—and had a very nice chat. He was a reserved man, with a kinky beard and stupidly small glasses. Great listener. I'd had a drink or two, and he wasn't saying much, so eventually I started talking about my problems. Maybe he'd be able to assist me, seeing how he belonged to the psychiatric profession. "Psychology," he corrected me, while nodding somewhat tiredly. I was guarded and euphemistic at first, but the gates had been opened, and soon it was all gushing out. All my life, I said, I'd been plagued by the most horrendously disjointed spontaneous thoughts. There were days where every flab of cloth brought to mind breasts and genitalia. Times when I couldn't clap eyes on another human without thinking of cannibalism. Not to mention the tangled grottiness of the putrid sexual images that sometimes plagued me.

What I found devastating weren't the thoughts per se. Those were, after all, just thoughts. The horrid thing was the fear that accompanied them: a terrible dread that they might be a symptom of some hidden impulse. That they betrayed an evil nested within me, like a snake coiled around my organs.

The man kept nodding through my explanation. "Sounds like obsessive-compulsive disorder," he said once I was finished. That struck me as preposterous. I thought that the term only applied to those blokes who need to put away their Monopoly with all the houses and hotels precisely right in the box. "The mind fixates on things," he continued, "and associates images, often of a violent or repulsive nature, with certain stimuli. In cases of obsessive disorder, these correlations can become calcified in place, and cause great distress. If you find them bothersome, talk to your GP. They'll recommend therapy or anxiolytics."

And that was it. All those years I'd been carrying that worry inside me, and this silly sod came along and put a name to it, and explained it away. It staggers me that we all walk around with the solution to each other's problems stored away within us, in our experiences and in the lessons we've learned, and yet we have not come up with any efficient system for sharing this knowledge. Except for books, I suppose. And who reads books these days?

I lived off tea for two days. When I felt that I could hold it down, I made a soup out of those carrots and potatoes in the cupboard. (The leek had sprouted a yellow beard, and I thought it best to avoid it.) It was thin and bland, but it tasted like life. I struggle to remember a meal I enjoyed more in recent years. Perhaps the last time Melvin and I ate out, at a sausage pub in Jericho called The Big Bang, his favorite place in the world. (They closed shortly after he died, his frequent patronage the only thing keeping them afloat.) We had some marvelous turnip mash, milky and velvety, with salt crystals peppered across its surface to pack a little burst of flavor with every forkful. We laughed, we joked, we ate to our bursting point. It was a good night.

It took all my self-control not to devour all the soup in one sitting. I poured two thirds of it in plastic containers, and stored them in the fridge for tomorrow's meals. This felt so cruel that I ended up sulking at my own wisdom.

All through the day I'd been scouring the oven with my most aggressive cleaning products, breathing in their toxic vapors, determined to erase all traces of poison. When I woke up the next morning I sighed, took out the flour, and baked the tiniest loaf of my life. I had a quarter of it for lunch. My bowels did not liquefy.

I finished the loaf that night with the second portion of soup. I slept like a baby, and woke up feeling rejuvenated. My oven was back in business. Everything would be all right.

I walked out into the garden to deal with the dead magpies. I shouldn't have left it so long, but I was hoping a fox would take them out of my hands. I guess foxes are too clever to eat poisoned birds. Or perhaps they all went wherever it is that 999 has gone.

I pulled on my thick plastic gloves and stuffed the slimy birds in a binbag. Not that my bins had been emptied at any time in the recent past. Kipfel was still in there, a disturbing and potentially dangerous fact I was doing a great job of ignoring. (A fun fact about the human mind: legitimate concerns are so much easier to dismiss than irrational fears.)

When I got up, with some difficulty, from leaning forward over the second bird, I saw a line of ducks, seven or eight of them, staring at me from beyond the fence.

My eyes darted to the door, and I saw that the outside of the cat flap, which I'd taped shut, was covered in scratches and dents. Beak marks.

I charged at the ducks, who scattered around the field, quacking indignantly as they took off. I took the dead magpies out of the binbag and threw them at the enemy. I missed. The magpies are still out there, by now little more than untroubled tufts of feathers and bones.

I asked Peter how dangerous ducks could be. He said that duck farmers contract salmonella a few times a year as a matter of course. When I pressed him for more information—how did they fare in *conventional* warfare?—he got unpleasant, and evasive.

Peter is the editor of the *International Review of Poultry Studies.* You'd think he should know about ducks. But his area of expertise is geese.

Academics, in my experience, tend to embrace the view that their superior knowledge of their field of study, the fact that they're such valuable members of society, excuses them from adhering to most societal norms—of politeness, responsiveness, punctuality. But for all that they're such geniuses they can't even tell you how actually dangerous a sodding duck can be.

The day after our confrontation in the garden, the ducks came into my house again.

I heard a scuttling noise at dawn, too loud for me to pretend it was outside. I made my way down the stairs, and saw muddy prints along the hall. They headed, unsurprisingly, into the kitchen, but I followed them the other way, to their source. The ducks had pushed up one of the sash windows in Carl's bedroom, and trailed mud across the bed and carpet.

I lost it. I ran into the kitchen, where three ducks were tearing at the half loaf I'd left under a cloth on the counter. I picked up the cloth from the floor and whipped them, forgetting the old wisdom about cornered animals.

They took flight, brushing past me on their way out. I covered my face. My arms got scratched. I'm not sure if they attacked me deliberately, or if their feet simply grazed me as they went by.

They flew down the hall and out the window, which I slammed closed, and locked. I collapsed on Carl's muddy bed, and spent a long time studying my scratches.

☉

Carl was our son. He always had a strong sense of justice, and he was passionate about music. He was in a band in high school that only played covers of this rock group called the Stiff Little Fingers, a name I always found enormously rude, even though it actually isn't. Melvin used to give him a hard time about that band. "Your songs are terrible," he would say, "and they're not even *yours*."

Carl had a few girlfriends, held a few jobs, but never anything serious. He had a car accident during a trip to Italy when he was thirty, and died.

I think about Carl the same way I think about my neuroses. It's all part of life. I say to myself that thirty years on Earth are not nothing: that during that time, Carl was loved, and frequently happy. But it's like telling myself that my anxieties are a condition, unfortunate but documented, endurable. It makes it bearable, most of the time; but the sorrow never goes away.

Melvin was never cruel to me, never *actively* nasty, but a couple of times, when I was trying to explain the nature of my anxieties to him—the obstinacy of my morbid thoughts—he replied in a way that wounded me deeply. "You Germans," he said, too exasperated by his own impossible problems to know how to deal with mine. "Always obsessed with cruelty."

☉

I baked a fresh loaf. I locked all the windows except for one, in the living room.

Two days later, at the first light of dawn, I heard the ducks push that window up and drop onto the floor. They were stealthier this time, and made very little noise as they waddled down the hall.

I left my hiding spot on top of the stairs and sneaked toward the kitchen. I found them clustered around my bread, which they'd dragged to the floor.

I lunged forward and closed my hand around a duck's neck. A female. She thrashed her wings and paddled with her feet in the air, trying perhaps to tear at my skin. Her resistance only increased my determination, making it easier to be forceful with her. I clutched her under my arm, immobilizing her, and took the kitchen knife out of my robe's pocket.

Her companions had stopped eating and were quacking furiously at me. They seemed paralyzed between flight and violence. I looked down at them with great hate, and they looked up at me with whatever they had inside them— duck faces always seem to express blunt annoyance.

I have to do it, I thought. These pests need to go. They'll give me salmonella. Steal all my bread. The first step of my extermination plan was a few millimeters away: the tip of my knife was resting on the duck's breast, and she was struggling less frantically every second, perhaps because I was squeezing her too hard.

And yet my mind was at work with a lucidity I'd never known before. I was trying desperately to come up with a solution that did not involve bloodshed. How ironic, after a lifetime plagued by violent and repulsive thoughts, to find out I was incapable of inflicting harm—and by ironic I mean sodding preposterous.

These ducks are hungry, I thought. They must have gotten addicted to carbs from all the bread they were fed when people were still allowed outside their house. I had flour. I had bread. I could keep it all to myself, sure: but what for? To keep living indefinitely in my inescapable house, seeing the world around me shut down bit by bit, carrying on throughout it all with my irrelevant, menial job?

I dropped my prisoner. She was flying before she'd even touched the floor. I didn't try to cover my face, but nobody scratched me on their way out.

Things got weird after that.

It wasn't the following day, and to be honest I couldn't say exactly how long after our confrontation this was—my mind was sluggish for a few days, probably as a comedown from that adrenaline burst in the kitchen—but eventually the ducks appeared again. They sat in a wonky semicircle outside my front door.

They must have seen that I was a softie. I baked a loaf, crumbled it up, and brought it out. How they knew this one wasn't poisoned is beyond me.

There are two encampments around my house, one in

the back garden, one on the front lawn. I tried to count the ducks in both, and reached a total of fifteen, but the figure is insignificant, as ducks come and go, and the camps seem to swell some days, and to be nearly abandoned on others.

I bake a loaf every two days, and hand it out in the morning. You'd think the ducks would have figured the schedule out, and perhaps they have, but either way they stay out there all the time, even on non-feeding days.

I'm well aware they might simply be keeping an eye on me. Making sure I do not leave.

How in the world, you may ask, do you still have enough flour to feed all these ducks. That's the weirdest part. I was running low on strong flour, and would have soon been forced to use plain flour for my bread (civilization truly is collapsing) when one night, after sunset, the ducks on my front lawn started quacking very loud.

I got out and showed them my bare hands—no bread until tomorrow morning!—but they turned around and started walking down the street. Once they reached the corner, they turned and called again.

There are only a handful of houses and cottages in Binsey, plus a pub, The Perch, whose late-night crowds of posh revelers used to be the bane of my sleep. The ducks led me past my neighbors' homes. We were violating quarantine—well, *I* was—but there was no one around to rat me out.

We got to a house painted peach and white, with a half-timbered first floor. Fancy. The ducks quacked for me to swing open the gate in the picket fence, and they guided me to the back garden.

The kitchen window had been opened, doubtlessly with the same burglary skills I'd already witnessed. It was close enough to the back door that I could reach my arm in, turn the key in the lock, and walk inside. Nobody was home, and there was no car in the driveway. I remembered two ghastly BMWs, and assumed that the owners must have fled to some even grander manor, deeper into the countryside.

The ducks tapped the cupboard under the sink with their beaks. Inside, I found a dozen 1.5 kg bags of stockpiled flour. Organic and local: the good stuff.

Most of the food in the fridge had spoiled, but I shopped freely from the cupboards. I left the backdoor open on my way out. Let the squirrels go crazy.

The cars still drive along the A34 whenever I go into my attic to check. (Have there been fewer of them recently? Hard to tell.) Peter still replies to my emails, although with less gusto and grease than before. Some of my colleagues have started showing up at the virtual tea breaks again. The ducks are hungry. I don't feel lonely.

CONTRIBUTORS

D Thea Baldrick

As a professional career changer, D. Thea Baldrick's experiences are kaleidoscopic. She has two Bachelor's degrees: a B.A. in Comparative Literature and a B.S. in Biology with a Concentration in Molecular and Cellular Biology. She attended George Washington Law School and spent twenty years homeschooling her children.

Usually residing in Ohio, she lived briefly in Madrid, traveled solo through Europe and occasionally inhabits imaginary landscapes with her grandchildren. She has worked in education, libraries, bookstores, and industries; most recently, as a microbiology technician in a soap company testing for microbial growth. Currently, she writes nonfiction about diseases and poets, and fiction about witches. Sometimes the topics overlap.

Portals to D.Thea's publications are at dthea.com

Ben Curl

Ben Curl writes speculative fiction when he's not writing damning letters to employers on behalf of union members.

His short stories have appeared as podcasts on *Horror Hill* and *Night Shift Radio*. "The Glass Folio," a tale about a nineteenth-century thief's obsession with a grotesque book that promises immortality, will appear in *Dark Horses: The Magazine of Weird Fiction* in the summer of 2022.

Many of his stories are inspired by self-guided and never-successful ghost hunts amid abandoned mineshafts and karsts in Michigan's Upper Peninsula.

He resides in Lansing, Michigan. You can follow him at ben-curl.com or on Twitter @BenjaminCurl

Scott Edelman

Scott Edelman has published more than 100 short stories in magazines such as *Analog, PostScripts, The Twilight Zone,* and *Dark Discoverie*s, and in anthologies such as *Why New Yorkers Smoke, MetaHorror, Crossroads: Southern Tales of the Fantastic, Once Upon a Galaxy, Moon Shots, Mars Probes,* and the Harlan Ellison tribute anthology *The Unquiet Dreamer.*

His collection of zombie fiction, *What Will Come After,* was published in 2010, and was a finalist for both the Stoker Award and the Shirley Jackson Memorial Award. His most recent collection, *Things That Never Happened,* was published in 2020. He has been a Bram Stoker Award finalist eight times, in the categories of Short Story and Long Fiction.

Additionally, Edelman worked for the Syfy Channel for more than thirteen years as editor of *Science Fiction Weekly, SCI FI Wire,* and *Blastr.* He was the founding editor of *Science Fiction Age,* which he edited during its entire eight-year run. He also edited *SCI FI magazine,* previously known as *Sci-Fi Entertainment,* as well as two other SF media magazines, *Sci-Fi Universe* and *Sci-Fi Flix.* He has also been a four-time Hugo Award finalist for Best Editor.

A. P. Howell

A. P. Howell lives with her spouse and their two kids, sometimes near a lake and always near trees. She has a master's degree in history and her jobs have spanned the alphabet from archivist to webmaster.

Her short fiction has appeared in a variety of places, including *Daily Science Fiction, Little Blue Marble, Martian: The Magazine of Science Fiction Drabbles, Translunar Travelers Lounge, In Somnio: A Collection of Modern Gothic Horror* (Tenebrous Press), and *Los Suelos, CA* (Surface Dweller Studios). She can be found online at aphowell.com or tweeting @APHowell.

W. T. Paterson

W. T. Paterson is a three-time Pushcart Prize nominee, holds an MFA in Fiction Writing from the University of New Hampshire, and is a graduate of Second City Chicago. His work has appeared in over 90 publications worldwide including *The Saturday Evening Post, The Forge Literary Magazine, The Delhousie Review, Brilliant Flash Fiction,* and *Fresh Ink.* A semi-finalist in the Aura Estra short story contest, his work has also received notable accolades from *Lycan Valley, North 2 South Press*, and *Lumberloft.* He spends most nights yelling for his cat to "Get down from there!"

Visit his website at www.wtpaterson.com.

Mattia Ravasi

Mattia Ravasi is from Monza, Italy, and lives and works in Oxford. He has written for *The Millions, Modern Fiction Studies,* and *The Submarine.* His stories have appeared in independent magazines, most recently in the *Wilderness House Literary Re-*

view, Flash Fiction Magazine, and *Planet Scumm*. He talks about books on his YouTube channel, *The Bookchemist*.

Mike Robinson

A writer since age six, Mike Robinson is the award-winning author of ten books, including the dark fantasy trilogy *Enigma of Twilight Falls* and the short story collection *Too Much Dark Matter, Too Little Gray*. His work has sold to Audible, and his short fiction has appeared in over twenty outlets. A lifelong resident of Los Angeles, he is a charter member of GLAWS (Greater Los Angeles Writers Society) as well as a screenwriter and producer. In between, he is a freelance literary editor, hiker, doodler, tries to play baseball again and keeps his two dogs smiling.

Eric Witchey

Eric Witchey has sold stories under several names and in 12 genres. His tales have been translated into multiple languages, and his credits include over 160 stories, including 5 novels and two collections. He has penned dozens of writing-related articles and essays, has taught over 200 conference seminars, at 2 universities, and at a community college. His work has received recognition from New Century Writers, *Writers of the Future, Writer's Digest*, Independent Publisher Book Awards, International Book Awards, The Eric Hoffer Prose Award Program, Short Story America, the Irish Aeon Awards, and other organizations. His How-to articles have appeared in *The Writer Magazine, Writer's Digest Magazine,* and other print and online magazines.

PAMELA COLMAN SMITH

The tarot images in this issue of Arcana are from the deck illustrated by Pamela Colman Smith. It was released in 1909 as the Rider-Waite deck (so named, at that time, in reference to its publisher, William Rider & Son). It remains the most influential and widely used tarot deck. While the impetus for the deck came from Arthur Edward Waite, Colman Smith was responsible for the iconography of the cards.

Pamela Colman Smith also illustrated over twenty books, wrote two collections of Jamaican folklore, edited two magazines, and ran the Green Sheaf Press, a small press devoted to women writers. She continued to write and illustrate throughout her life.

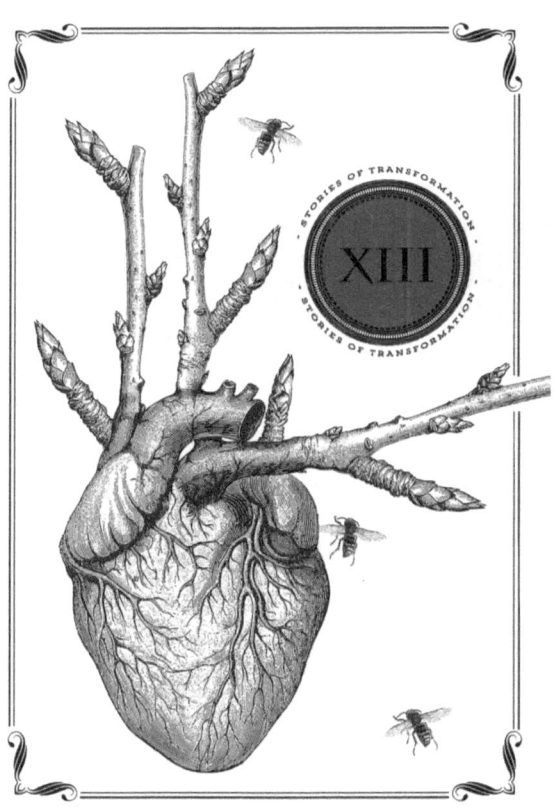

STORIES OF TRANSFORMATION

XIII

STORIES OF TRANSFORMATION

XIII

The thirteenth Tarot card is Death, and he is a symbol not of the end, but of transformation and rebirth. This is the genesis and root of *Thirteen: Stories of Transformation*. The twenty-eight authors of this collection are voices—new and old—who are not afraid to explore what comes next. Whether it be a life after death, a life without love, a life filled with hunger, or the life shared by a ghost. These are stories of the weird, the mythic, the fantastic, the futuristic, the supernatural, and the horrific.

With stories by Liz Argall • M. David Blake • Richard Bowes • George Cotronis • Amanda C. Davis • Julie C. Day • Jetse de Vries • Jennifer Giesbrecht • Daryl Gregory • Rik Hoskin • Rebecca Kuder • Claude Lalumière • Marc Levinthal • Grá Linnaea • Alex Dally MacFarlane • Juli Mallett • Lyn McConchie • Fiona Moore • Gregory L. Norris • Adrienne J. Odasso • Cat Rambo • Andrew Penn Romine • David Tallerman • Tais Teng Richard Thomas • Fran Wilde • A. C. Wise • Christie Yant

Edited by Mark Teppo.

Available at independent bookstores everywhere.

http://www.underlandpress.com

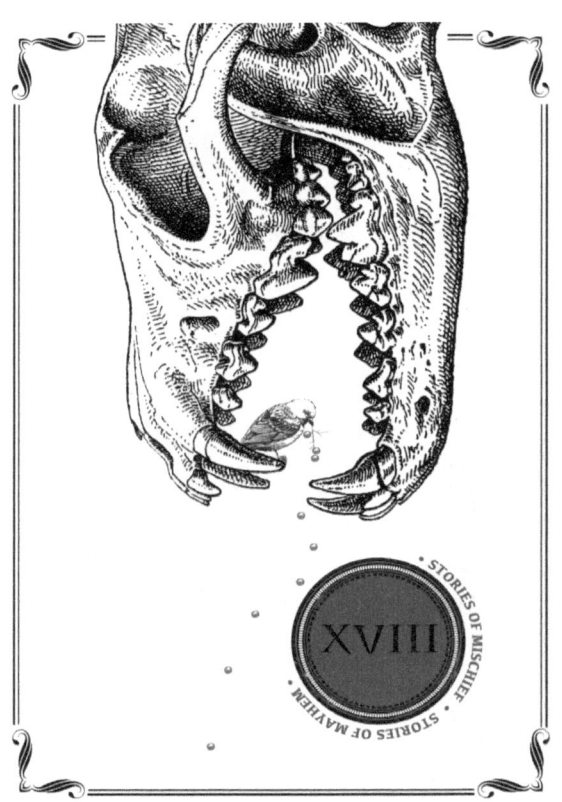

XVIII

XVIII

The eighteenth Tarot card is the Moon, and those who raise their arms to her know she offers Mercy and Severity in equal measure. This is the great river at night, where wolves howl and all doors are open. All futures are possible, and every truth is elusive. This is the source and passion of *Eighteen: Stories of Mischief & Mayhem*. These twenty-four stories from voices—old and new—celebrate the inevitability of fate, the horror of prophecy, and the shivering delight of not knowing what comes next.

Cross over the threshold with us, and explore the strange, the weird, and the fantastic. Do not fear what lies ahead. It is the same as what came before. The only difference is you. This is *Eighteen*, and nothing will be the same.

With stories by Forrest Aguirre • Darin Bradley • Christopher East • Scott Edelman • Nicole Feldringer • Ben Gamblin • Ingrid Garcia • A. P. Howell • Emma Johnson-Rivard • E. E. King • Jessie Kwak • Shannon Lawrence • Gerri Leen • Mark Mills • Christi Nogle Tammie Painter • Josh Rountree • Erica Sage • Lorraine Schein • J. Dee Stanley • Richard Thomas • John Waterfall • Wendy N. Wagner • Todd Zack

Edited by Mark Teppo.

Available at independent bookstores everywhere.

http://www.underlandpress.com